Vanisher

Chronicles of the Warren

Vanisher

Chronicles of the Warren
A Novel

Tom Grimwood

OUR STREET
BOOKS

London, UK
Washington, DC, USA

CollectiveInk

First published by Our Street Books, 2025
Our Street Books is an imprint of Collective Ink Ltd.,
Unit 11, Shepperton House, 89 Shepperton Road, London, N1 3DF
office@collectiveinkbooks.com
www.collectiveinkbooks.com
www.Ourstreet-Books.com

For distributor details and how to order please visit the 'Ordering' section on our website.

Text copyright: Tom Grimwood 2023

ISBN: 978 1 80341 729 5
978 1 80341 739 4 (ebook)
Library of Congress Control Number: 2023951109

A CIP catalogue record for this book is available from the British Library.

Design: Lapiz Digital Services

UK: Printed and bound by CPI Group (UK) Ltd, Croydon, CR0 4YY
Printed in North America by CPI GPS partners

We operate a distinctive and ethical publishing philosophy in all areas of our business, from our global network of authors to production and worldwide distribution.

Prologue

The land of Bryvania had, at one time, been wild and savage. Small clusters of civilised settlements – humans, elves, even dwarves at one point – were surrounded by vast mountain ranges, deep forests and endless plains, occupied by hosts of strange and often deadly creatures, warlords, dark magicians and worse. And, above all, Bryvania was full of adventure. Adventurers wandered the land, daring to brave towers, dungeons, mazes and citadels all in the search of gold and glory.

But that was all long ago. And once there were less deadly creatures to fight, and fewer villages to save, and the use of magic was outlawed, and there was far less treasure to seek, Bryvania had a problem. There were too many adventurers, and not enough adventures. And where there were adventurers, there were traders, armourers, taverns ... as the cities grew, the lords and nobles began to realise that evil had been removed in all but the darkest corners of the land. And this concerned them.

While some attempted to offer different paths for the young adventurers – joining their household as guards, learning other skills – none of these seemed to match the allure of gold and glory. But one lord, the scheming Baron of Kaveshvill, had a different plan.

He created the Warren. The Warren was a vast underground complex of caves and tunnels, built upon an ancient dungeon ruled by a dark wizard, which in turn was built on an even more ancient set of caves from a time nobody knew of. Somewhere deep within the Warren, the myth went, was a chamber full of more gold than the world had ever seen. Possibly guarded by a dragon.

Whether the dragon was real or not didn't matter, because the Baron filled the Warren with as many creatures, worldly and unworldly, as he could find. He offered areas as homes to

1

goblins and drows, and lich and kobolds took refuge in others. It was rumoured that the deeper the Warren went, the stronger the elemental forces were, and magicians who had been driven from their towers and castles entered the Warren to attempt to regain their power.

And then, the Baron opened the Warren to adventurers.

He built a citadel, which he called Skala, on top of the seven entrances to the Warren. He then charged adventurers to once again risk their lives in the name of fame and fortune by descending into the infinite levels of the dungeon below. There were some regulations, of course: those adventurers who re-emerged from the Warren carrying gold found that any attempt to leave Skala had a heavy tax applied, and the gold itself was such an old currency that it was little use in the outside world. But most adventurers had no reason to leave. Skala had plenty of entertainments to occupy them, should they be successful in the Warren. And if they weren't successful ... well, they wouldn't be in any state to leave.

And, of course, there was the Rule of One. The Warren was a place of individual heroism, and once inside, there was to be no collaboration, no working with others, no helping the unfortunate. This was to be the ultimate test of fighting skill, and as the minstrels of Skala sang every night, the test was faced alone.

So the lords and nobles of Bryvania were happy, for now the adventurers had a place to go that wasn't in their own cities. The adventurers were happy, because they could find work. And the Baron became very rich. Skala became known as the citadel of adventure, and when the Baron died, his son, the new Baron, built a palace there which would become the envy of the land. The legends and mysteries of the Warren grew, along with the power and influence of the new Baron.

Until, one day, somebody came up with a plan to bring it all down. And this is where our story begins....

1

The girl in the shadows

The streets of Blackwater were quiet, or at least quieter than the throng and clatter of the daytime. The smell of the market never quite went away, of course – the fish, the spices, and the undoubted sense of illegal activities – but the traders, sailors and brigands were now residing in taverns. The streets were populated only with the odd guard, a beggar or two, and the shadows.

In one such shadow, a girl named Azra was standing, very still. She waited, watching the houses, the windows, listening for any sound of danger. Even at this time of night, she needed to make sure that nobody would see her. In her hand, she held a piece of parchment that had been left at her house, back in her village, a few days ago. It had told her to be at a particular house in Blackwater on this night, and that her attendance would be rewarded beyond what she could imagine. She had no idea where it had come from, or how they knew where she lived. Her village was hardly on the map, just a small fishing settlement which nobody came to and nobody left. And even there, nobody much spoke to her, especially after the ... accidents.

Which was why the note had led her here, to Blackwater, the furthest she had ever been from her home. Not because of the promise of riches – although that sounded great – but because of the sentence that followed. The note had said: *I have particular use for someone with your skills. You will no longer have to hide them.*

A noise on the street made her step back against the wall, concealed from view as two guards walked past.

'What was all that about in the Black Lion? A right disturbance,' one of the guards was saying.

'Oh, some card trick getting out of hand,' the other replied. 'They said someone was doing magic in the pub.'

'Magic? I don't like the sound of that...'

'Pfft, sounded more like some con artist had taken some punter's money, so they smashed the place up. It's been a long time since we've seen an actual magician in these parts.'

'Yeah, well let's keep it that way. We don't want any crime lords moving in. Magic is illegal for a reason...'

They disappeared off around the corner. Azra went tense at the mention of magic. The guards couldn't mean her, surely? But she hadn't been to any pub. In fact, after sneaking away from her village, she had travelled along the coast and come straight to this part of the town, keeping to the shadows, keeping out of sight, and when needed ... disappearing.

She continued to watch the street. Across from her was a house, no different in size and shape to any other in Blackwater. Azra had been watching it for the last hour. While the flicker of candlelight coming from inside suggested habitation, she had so far seen nobody enter or leave. Carefully, she unfolded the parchment she had carried with her from her village, and, using the light of the moon, focused on the last line. *Come to Harbour Way, the third house from the postern gate, at the tenth hour.*

At that moment, the sound of a bell chiming carried its way across the drowsy town. Ten o'clock.

Azra heard someone approaching. In fact, it was difficult not to hear them – they clanked up the street, a broadsword clattering against ill-fitting shirt of chain mail. This was an older man, big and burly – very big, in fact, and Azra wondered if he may be some kind of giant. The man stopped at the third house, looked around expectantly, sniffed the air, and went to march straight in, not bothering to knock. He looked surprised when the door opened before he had a chance to kick it. After only a brief pause, he stalked inside.

4

No sooner had the door closed, Azra became aware of someone else in the street. They were moving quietly, but experience in the village – hiding from the elders when she had her 'accidents' – had taught her to listen for even the softest of sounds, and so she had detected the figure long before they came into view. It was a boy of her age, perhaps no more than sixteen, who walked quickly – upright and purposeful, as though confident, but also looking from side to side, suggesting that they may not know quite where they were. Certainly, his clothes, which seemed to be of good material like the nobility wore, suggested he was not used to walking the streets of Blackwater. But there was something else about him that stood out. Even though he wore a hat which covered his ears, his elegant posture and deft movement made his true identity unmistakable. *He's an elf,* she thought, *he must be an elf.* No wonder he looks so worried about being in a human town.

Almost as soon as she thought it, the elf turned around, staring straight across at the doorway where Azra hid. He peered into the shadows. 'Who's there?' he called. 'Show yourself!'

Of course, elves also had sharper senses, Azra thought, and kept as still as she could to remain unseen. But the elf kept looking and, reaching for a sword hanging from his belt, began to step across the street towards her. Azra felt her hands warm, and instinctively closed her eyes. She felt a shiver go through her entire body, and in a moment she found herself perched on a shop sign, which hung high above her previous hiding place. The elf was below her, peering at the doorway.

'Must have been nothing,' he said, shaking his head. 'Calm yourself, Sylvindor…'

And with that, he returned to the house across the street. Checking a piece of parchment in his hand, he tentatively went to the door. It opened for him, before he could knock – and he went inside.

'Two others,' thought Azra to herself. 'Did they all receive an invitation like me, I wonder? And what a strange group so far.'

Well, she had come this far. There was no point in continuing to wait. Checking again that the street was empty, she jumped down from the sign on to the street below, and stepped forward towards the house…

A sword flashed in front of her, hovering dangerously close to her face.

'And what are you doing?' a woman's voice said.

Azra froze. Her heart raced, and she began to feel that strange itchy feeling in her hands which usually meant an … accident… was going to happen. The guards must have seen her! She tried to breathe and remain calm. She couldn't give any indication she could do magic. Concentrating hard on making her hands return to normal, she turned to look up at the swordswoman.

But it was not a guard. She was dressed more like an adventurer, or at least what Azra assumed an adventurer would dress like.

'What are you doing?' she asked again.

'Wh—why should I tell you? What business is it of yours?' Azra stammered.

'I have a sword to your throat, so it's my business,' the woman said, raising an eyebrow.

Azra considered that this was a good enough reason. She gulped. 'I'm … going to that house over there.'

'Are you? The house you have been watching for the last hour?'

Azra must have been visibly surprised by this, and the woman went on: 'Oh yes, you're good – very sneaky, if I may say. But I'm better. I don't even need to use vanishing tricks. So I now wonder … what's your name…?'

The sword in front of her suggested to Azra that she should tell the truth.

'Azra,' she replied.

'So now I wonder, Azra ... there are two reasons one might watch a house for so long. One is that you are a thief. Are you a thief?'

Azra considered. The answer was perhaps more complicated than she'd like to say, and the itching in her hands and the woman's sword were not letting her think all that clearly.

'But I suppose if you were a thief, why would you go to the house when three people have just entered?' the woman went on. 'So it must be the second reason. That you have one of these.'

She put her sword down, and with her other hand presented a piece of parchment. Azra could not read it in the dim light, but could see it was written in the same hand as hers. She nodded.

The adventurer sheathed her sword. 'Well then, Azra. As we are here for the same reason, perhaps we should go in together?'

The sense in her hands subsided. Azra relaxed a little, and nodded.

'Good. You can call me Quil. I don't know what this meeting is about, and I don't trust it at all. But so far you've shown more sense than any of the others, so stick with me and perhaps we can make sense of this.'

Quil held out her hand, and Azra, somewhat surprised, shook it.

'Now, let's go in...'

2

A strange meeting

The door opened before them, although nobody seemed to be there. As they stepped into the house, cautiously, a little old woman emerged from behind the door, and motioned for them to go through to the back of the house.

They entered a room that was sparsely furnished, with a long table and one or two dressers. At the table sat the two people Azra had seen entering before – the young elf and the giant – and at the far end sat another woman, who had long dark hair which hung straight over her tunic. She was elegant, Azra thought, but had a strange intensity which seemed to project across the room and on to all who sat there. This was clearly *her* meeting. But for now, she said nothing, simply sat with her fingers resting against each other. Everyone else was silent too.

'I suppose we can sit down?' said Quil, gruffly. She kicked out the nearest chair and, without waiting for a reply, sat down, resting her feet on the next seat along. She glanced up at Azra and, with a quick flick of her head, indicated she should sit down as well.

There was another moment of silence.

'Well?' Quil raised her eyebrows. 'What is this all about? Or do we just sit here without saying anything?'

The elegant woman did nothing, but a smile crept across her face. 'We are waiting for one more.'

'Perhaps he ain't coming,' the little old woman, who had just bustled in with a jug of water for the table, muttered to herself. 'You don't know he'll come, do you? And it's just like those tricksters to not...'

'Oh, he'll come,' the woman interrupted her, in a calm, measured tone. 'In fact ... I wonder if he isn't already here.'

There was a sudden gust of wind from nowhere, and Azra instinctively looked to the door, but it was still shut. Then a moment of darkness swept past her, and before she knew any of what had happened, she found a man sat on the other side of the table to her.

'Impressive,' nodded Quil, although she didn't sound too impressed. 'Couldn't you just use the door like the rest of us?'

The man grinned back at her. He had a slightly disfigured face, and the shadows from the candlelight danced across it, seeming to turn it this way, then that. There was the look in his eye of one who had seen more than most could dream of; but also the guile and cunning of one who knows to keep such things secret.

'There are so many more *interesting* ways to enter a room,' he said. 'Why all use the same way?'

Quil turned away from him, back to the woman.

'A trickster,' she said, with some disdain. 'A trickster, a thug, a boy and a...' she thumbed back towards Azra, 'well, a half-decent thief, I suppose ... What do you all need us for here, exactly?'

The woman put her hands down on the table. '*Adventure*, my friends. Adventure.'

The company exchanged wary looks with each other. What did she mean?

'I suppose it might be best to start by lifting some of this mystery and introducing myself,' the woman said. 'My name is Vane. And I, like you all, long for adventure.'

'You seem very sure of what we want,' the trickster interrupted, and he waved a parchment – similar to the one Azra had received – in the air. 'There are a lot of promises in this invitation, and I was rather hoping that adventure wasn't one of them.'

'Master Sekobi, adventure is precisely what you long for. Oh, you may find some enjoyment in card tricks and illusions in taverns, taking people's money until the guards chase you to the next town. But it is not adventure. And you, Marsali Quil, you may find some coin as a sword for hire these days, but it's not the life you once had.'

These names stirred something in Azra's memory, but she wasn't sure what. Vane continued, pointing to the elf. 'Sylvindor Fennan, disinherited from his tree village, and cast out into the wider world. A world which hates elves, and hates poor elves even more. So who will notice your amazing speed? Your quickness with the sword and bow? Remarkable skills, if you were ever to be allowed to put them to the test.'

The boy went red. 'I'm not sure what that has to do with anything...' he said, indignantly, but Azra thought he sounded quite hurt.

'Or Grug Terok. A fine bodyguard once. Probably still a fine fighter, I would suppose. But now your lord is dead and nobody needs a mutant half-giant.'

Grug looked angry, and clenched his massive fists.

'And, of course, Azra Mujkic. Despised by your village because of those... mishaps... that seem to happen all around you. How you seem to be able to affect the very elements which surround us all. Some even say you can vanish and reappear in a different place, almost as if you were... *magical*.'

'They're just accidents,' said Azra, suddenly very uncomfortable. 'I'm not...'

'My friends,' Vane continued, ignoring her, 'you are all made for adventure. It calls you, as it calls me. And I have the perfect adventure for us all.'

'If you want adventure, go to the Warren,' said Sekobi with a shrug. 'Now, I'm glad to have made all these new friends tonight, but really, I have to go.'

'Oh, I *intend* to go to the Warren,' said Vane. 'But not to play the Baron's silly games. Not to carry on this charade of adventure he has created. Oh no. What I have brought you here for is the greatest challenge of all.' She glanced quickly to make sure the doors were closed before lowering her voice. 'To destroy the Warren.'

There was a moment's silence.

'What I mean is, fulfil every adventurer's dream and *beat the Warren*. Steal its riches, bring down its myth, and make us all ... Very. Rich. Indeed.'

3

The plan

There was a long pause. Then Sekobi said: 'You're mad. Nobody beats the Warren.'

'And why not?' asked Vale. 'We have the two greatest adventurers to ever step foot in the place right here. Nobody has journeyed deeper, or survived for longer, than you.'

And she looked straight ahead at Azra, who was confused, until Vale turned her head from side to side, indicating she was actually talking about Quil and Sekobi.

Of course, Azra thought, that was where she had heard the names before. She caught her breath, and for a moment her hands started to warm and itch.

'Then it really is you!' blurted out the elf. 'I can't believe it – I've heard so many stories, I...'

Quil raised her hand, gently. 'That's enough, boy. All of that was a long time ago.'

'But you are famed warriors!' Sylvindor kept going. 'People would talk about you at all the feasts, and how you ... how you fought the dragon, and how you...'

Quil fixed him with a hard stare. '*Enough*,' she said, firmly.

'If you're really Sekobi and Quil,' grunted the giant, 'then you must be the richest people alive already. Why are you here?'

Sekobi had been occupied at this point, glancing curiously at Azra's hands, but now he looked over to Grug and said: 'No. Don't you understand? Inside Skala, yes, gold, jewels, so much I've taken from those caves. All inside Skala. But there's no taking it out. It's a world inside those walls. If you find any gold, you must spend it inside the citadel – they won't let you leave with it.'

'And the only thing to spend it on is going back inside the Warren,' Quil agreed. 'Buy this special armour here! Buy this magical sword here! And back you go, into the Warren, back and forth. Until you die.'

'But you're both still alive...' protested Sylvindor.

Sekobi folded his arms. 'Perhaps,' he said. Then he looked over to Vane. 'I've done my time there. I've played the Baron's game. But I'm not going back,' he said, flatly.

Vane gave him a strange half-smile. '*Of course* I know the dangers of the Warren. Believe me, I know almost everything there is to know about it. I know how the old Baron discovered the caves beneath his dungeons and filled them with whatever monsters he could find, letting them breed and infest everywhere. I know how he built the citadel of Skala above the dungeons as a haven for adventurers who were flooding the country at the time. I know Skala is a different world to the one we inhabit. I also know how many have died seeking their fortune down there.'

'Millions,' Quil spoke without exaggeration. 'But that much is history. People like you still think that it might be you, that everybody else might have missed something, right?' She sat back in her seat, unimpressed. '*Your* type never clear the first level.'

'I know other things,' Vane continued. 'And I know that the Warren runs on the assumption of individual interest. Everybody goes in alone, operates alone, and so dies alone. While everyone works against each other, the Warren prospers.'

'There are rules against working together,' said Quil. 'They are enforced ... harshly.'

Vane nodded. 'But what if – what if I told you that I knew a way out of the Warren.'

'You mean out of Skala?' said Sekobi.

'No, not through the citadel. A way out of the Warren from inside the caves, straight out to the real world.'

'You would be lying,' Quil was getting impatient. 'Such a way does not exist.'

'Imagine,' Vane went on. 'The old Baron's labyrinth was built on caves much older than he could imagine. Imagine that other such networks of tunnels exist, under the ground, within the mountains. Now, imagine a secret passage, concealed by magic, linking the Warren to another run of caves, which, traversed correctly, will eventually lead outside of the confines of the Baron's rule. And then – well, then you can stop imagining. For the gold ... is all yours.'

Silence. Azra wasn't quite sure whether to be in awe of this claim, or to not believe it. Vane, who seemed to like stopping for dramatic pauses, now continued.

'Here is my proposal, friends. I have selected you because you each hold a skill essential to my plan. So, we will work as a team. We enter the Warren and make our way through to the lowest levels. That is where the hordes of gold lie. But we'll be safe – relatively – by working as a group rather than individuals. We take the money, we find the secret passage, and we leave – with riches beyond our wildest dreams.'

Then, from her cloak, she produced a leather cylinder, which she carefully unclasped and pulled from it an old parchment. She laid it on the table, where all eyes fell on it.

It was evidently a map. But of where, it wasn't clear. Lines crossed and bent over the page, and it had but two words written too small and worn to recognise. The onlookers were silent.

'Well?' Grug was indifferent.

'That's what I thought at first,' Vane said, 'but I spent some time deciphering the names written. Here,' – she pointed to the word on the right-hand side of the parchment – 'this marks the village of Anson. A good few miles east of the Warren's limits. And this word here,' – she indicated a word across the page – 'this simply says "CAVE".'

'And from that you deduced it's a way out of the Warren?' Sekobi pulled a face. 'How would you know? Have you ever been inside the Warren?'

14

Vane held her poise, though Azra noticed her lip trembled ever so slightly. 'I have worked years on this plan, Master Sekobi. It has cost me everything.'

'Hang on.' Quil was examining the map, trying to follow the lines as though she was walking them. 'This here – see this? The sharp turn, then another, then these sort of indents on the line? That's unmistakable. I would only know that layout if I'd been there.'

She closed her eyes, and Azra could feel her thinking, thinking, trying to remember.

Now Sekobi was looking at the map too. At first, he seemed uninterested. But then, he started to trace a line with his finger, following lines that Azra could barely make out. And then Quil was nodding.

'This is a deep level,' she said. 'I know of no other adventurer to make it this far. I don't think I got any further than there myself.'

'I thought I was alone down there too,' said Sekobi. 'But my memory says it's a dead end.'

'Not a dead end,' said Vane. 'A door – hidden by magic.'

'A magic door?' asked Quil. 'Now I remember why I left adventuring … silly…'

'But…' Sekobi put his hand to his head, 'Now I think, I remember there was something strange about that area. Some kind of aura … I couldn't find what it was.'

'This mark,' Vane pointed, 'is a cryptic rune. For years I searched for its meaning, and eventually found it in an old wizard's tower, long abandoned. It shows a door, steeped in old magic. And this passageway, outside of the Warren, has only very recently been unearthed by some dwarven miners. Sadly, *they* did not survive the fall … but the way to the door remains open.'

'And the door itself?' asked Quil, raising a sharp eyebrow.

'It can be opened, with enough skill and force. The lower levels are steeped with magical energy. And besides, should it not be possible to open, there would still be ways to pass the gold through.' And Vane looked straight ahead at Azra.

Sekobi rubbed his eye. 'You're talking of teleportation now?'

Sylvain looked startled. 'You mean a … a *vanisher*…?'

'I have chosen you all for the unique skills you have to offer,' Vane replied, firmly. 'Together, we can break the Baron's hold on the Warren.'

'Enough about magic,' said Grug, impatiently. 'Where are all these riches coming from?'

'This is where our experienced friends come in.' Vane was smiling again. 'Listen, I have maps. I have maps of the first four levels.'

'How?' asked Quil. 'No maps can leave the citadel.'

But Vane produced another leather holder and from it pulled four larger parchments. She placed them in front of the adventurers.

'As I say, I have maps of these levels. And on level four, I believe that this staircase…' – she shuffled the pages until she found the right one – '…this staircase will take us as far down as we need to go.'

'Where do we need to go?'

'Where else? To the dragon's lair.'

4

Azra makes a decision

Enter the Warren, find a dragon's lair, steal its gold, leave through a magic door, Azra said to herself. What could be simpler than that?

'My friends, that is my plan,' Vane concluded. 'I will give you one hour to decide if you want to join me.'

'Good,' said Grug, standing up to leave. 'I need a drink.'

'Due to the ... necessary ... secrecy of this meeting, I would ask that you all stay in the house for that time.' Vane smiled politely at the half-giant. 'But I'm sure Hathred can find you some ale.'

The little old woman shuffled off to one of the back rooms. Grug huffed, and stomped into the room at the front of the house, his clanking armour telling them all where he was.

Sylvindor also got up, looking apologetic. 'I, er, I just need to...'

'Up the stairs, on the left,' smiled Vane. Then she gracefully moved to her feet. 'One hour, friends,' she said, and disappeared through a side door to the back of the house, leaving Azra with Sekobi and Quil at the table.

Sekobi stood up and stretched. Quil, who remained seated, looked up at him.

'I suppose I should say it's a ... it's interesting to meet the legendary Sekobi here,' she said. Then she narrowed her eyes. 'You are ... what I expected.'

'And you, Marsali Quil,' Sekobi replied. 'Though I imagined you as somebody grander, given your reputation. Of course, I had also heard you were dead.'

There was an uneasy pause.

'I think perhaps both our reputations were grander in the Warren,' Quil said, pushing her chair back to get up. She cast Sekobi another, distrusting look, before heading towards the front room, motioning with her hand for Azra to follow.

Azra also stood up, as Sekobi leaned against the wall, his arms folded. She hesitated slightly, which he noticed.

'I can teach you how to use it, you know,' he said.

'What do you mean?' Azra snapped back, defensively.

Sekobi nodded towards her hands. 'It's a marvellous gift. No doubt you've been told it's a curse. No doubt you've been chased out of a few places ... but used correctly, Azra, used *well* ... it's a marvellous gift.'

Sekobi had a strange, sing-song voice which Azra somehow found warming and dangerous at the same time. And before she was even aware that she wanted to leave, her hands burned, and in a snap she found herself in the front room of the house.

Grug was sat in the corner, peering out of the window shutters and slurping on a stein of beer. Quil was examining a bookcase.

'Oh, there you are,' she said. 'Interesting person, this Vane. She has quite the collection of books here.'

'Her ale is fine,' Grug mumbled to himself. Quil ignored this and turned to Azra.

'So, my little thief, what do you think?'

'I'm not sure,' Azra replied. 'I don't really know why I'm here. I'm not an adventurer or a warrior.'

'Yet our host seems to have reasons for inviting all of us. Doubtless she has a role worked out for you.'

'What about you?' Azra asked, also looking at the shelves. They seemed to be full of ancient volumes of various lost languages, and maps of long destroyed kingdoms.

Quil had pulled out one book, which looked like some kind of volume on werebeasts.

'I swore a long time ago to never go back to Skala,' she said. 'For all that it made me, it also destroyed me.'

'What do you mean?' Azra frowned.

Quil thumbed the pages. 'It's an addiction. The power, the wealth, the fame. And it's all meaningless. It's all just a game played by the Baron, and I was just a piece in the game.' Then she looked past the book, lost in thought. 'But to rob the Baron … to make him pay, finally…'

'MORE BEER!' shouted Grug, and from somewhere the little woman scuttled in with a pitcher.

Quil snapped the book shut. 'It has already destroyed me once, little thief. It will destroy you too. If I were you, I would steer well clear of this.'

She walked out, narrowly avoiding Sylvindor, who was wandering in looking for people.

'Are you going to do it?' he asked Azra, excitedly.

Azra shrugged. 'I don't know yet.'

From the corner, Grug belched loudly.

'What's to think about?' asked the elf, almost hopping up and down. 'Gosh, to travel with Marsali Quil and Sekobi – that would be the adventure to end all adventures!'

'They haven't agreed to it yet,' Azra pointed out.

'Well, no, but … well, they will. I think they will. All the same, what an adventure it would be. You know, I've always dreamed of going to the Warren, haven't you?'

Azra confessed that she hadn't. It had always seemed a long way away from her village, and besides, she still didn't see what use her 'skills' would be.

She passed the time with her new elf friend for a while. He was keen to talk, which was at least a nice change from the people she usually encountered. He told her of his home in the forest kingdom of Haemir, and how he had been cheated by his brother out of his rightful inheritance, and how he had since been making his own way. He was keen to suggest that he and Azra were similar, although she was certainly no elven prince, and not the swordfighter he claimed to be.

All the while, she was still turning over Vane's strange offer in her mind. She realised, as Grug emptied another pitcher, that the hour must soon nearly be up. Making a polite excuse, she made her way back to the room they had met in.

Sekobi was still there, sat cross-legged on the table.

'If you're looking for your adventurer, she's upstairs,' said Sekobi.

'Have you decided?' Azra asked.

Sekobi's lips curled into what might have been a smile. 'Perhaps.'

Azra sat down, looked at him and shrugged. She wasn't interested in wily games.

'Quil and I have spoken,' Sekobi said. 'We both agree that the plan is ridiculous, and has no chance of working. There is far more to lose than to gain.'

Azra narrowed her eyes. 'I don't believe you,' she said.

This time Sekobi smiled a proper smile. 'Just because I'm called the trickster, doesn't mean I never tell the truth. Still...' he swung his legs down and took a chair. 'I like you, thief. Think about what I said – I could teach you a lot. More than simple disappearing tricks.'

They were interrupted by others re-entering the room. Sylvindor and Grug – who was swaying slightly now – came in from the front of the house and took their seats, while Quil appeared from the stairs, sitting back down next to Azra and casting a deeply distrustful look across the table to Sekobi. Finally, Vane entered from the small door she had left, and resumed her place at the head of the table.

'So,' she began, in her low voice. 'You have had time to consider my proposal. What is it to be, my friends?'

Grug put his stein down, roughly. 'The plan is foolish,' he announced. 'I'm out.'

Vane did not react, but merely bowed her head slightly. 'Very well, master barbarian. I suspected that might be the case.'

Sylvindor looked genuinely surprised, and stuttered: 'W—well I'm in!' probably too quickly. Vane raised her eyebrows.

'Indeed, master elf.'

There was a pause. Vane looked across to Sekobi.

'And what of Sekobi the Trickster?'

Sekobi, in turn, looked across the table to Quil, then back to Vane. 'I'm in,' he said.

Azra felt Quil tense, and grind her jaw.

'Then I guess I'm in, too,' Quil growled. Azra realised at that point that Quil was not going to let Sekobi back into the Warren without her. Clearly, the risk of the plan was outweighed by the possibility of the other carrying it out successfully.

And this, Azra also realised, made up her mind for her. Perhaps Sekobi really could teach her how to use her skills properly. Perhaps Quil could teach her how to be an adventurer. Either way, as Vane looked at her for a response, she knew she could only nod. 'I'm in,' she said.

'Pah!' Grug shouted. 'You're all fools!' And he kicked back his chair and stood up to leave. But then, a strange look came over his face. His hand went to his neck, and his eyes went to the empty stein of beer. Then he started to gurgle and splutter, and finally whispered: 'Fools!' once more, before collapsing to the floor.

'Good,' said Vane, not even seeming to notice the dead half-giant. 'We shall put this plan into action.'

5

The Citadel

It was early morning, and the sun had only just climbed over the snow-capped peaks of the Screaming Mountains, casting jagged rays over the road that wound its way through the foothills. The road had only one destination: the citadel of Skala.

Azra had set off well before dawn, after an uncomfortable night in the woods. Even though she had arrived at Skala as early as possible, already a queue had formed at the citadel gates. Adventurers, of all shapes and sizes, were keenly awaiting their turn to enter. This, as Quil had warned them back in Blackwater, was a slow process; the citadel guards carried out a long series of checks and searches before anyone was allowed inside.

'They will look for any sign you are linked with someone else,' she had warned. 'Remember the Rule of One. In the Warren, every person is for themselves.'

Azra took her place at the back of the line, looking up at the jagged walls of white stone that were both magnificent and terrifying at the same time. Beyond the walls, the citadel was watched over by the tall spires of the Baron's palace, far in the distance.

'A bit young, aren't you?' a voice said. She turned around and saw a man with a weathered, unkind face formed by years of disgust for others. 'No place for kids here, girl.'

She glared back at him and felt her hands going warm. *Calm,* she thought, *stay calm.* Magic may be allowed inside the Warren, but it was still considered illegal here, and even within the streets of Skala.

'You don't look well prepared,' the man went on. He pointed at her belt. 'That sword will break in no time down in the caves.'

Again, Azra said nothing, even though she found this man very irritating. Sekobi had been teaching her control of what he called her 'power', and she focused on what he had said about remaining calm. 'Disappearing is your weapon,' he had said. 'But it's a weapon to use carefully. Shock and surprise – that's what will do the damage.'

'Or perhaps,' the man continued. 'You're one of those rich types who's going to buy the fancy gear before going in. Well, if that's the case, I'll be relieving you of your gold once we're down in the dungeons...'

At this point, the warrior standing in front of Azra finally turned around. 'Ah, leave it, Ganhaw,' they said. 'She's clearly here to work the taverns. Not everybody in the line is still seeking their fortune.'

'Another tourist, more like!' spat Ganhaw, angrily.

'How is your fortune these days, Ganhaw?' the warrior asked. 'Clearly it brings you back to the Warren again...'

'That's none of your business!' replied the vile man, and he shook his fist.

Azra turned away, deciding to use this as good practice for blocking out the world, as Sekobi had taught her. This, she considered, was a better use of time than putting into practice what Quil had taught her of swordplay.

After what seemed like an age, she made it to the gates. There, five huge guards, dressed in the black and silver chevron of the Baron's coat of arms, searched her and informed her of the rules of the city. She already knew these from Quil, and remained thinking about her training so far, giving nothing away to the guards as to what she was there for. Eventually they cleared her to enter, and she stepped through the citadel gates into a large plaza beyond.

She hung back for a moment by the gateway and heard the guards talking.

'That one won't be here long, probably won't make it past the entrance!'

'More blood for the Baron. So long as they spend their money before they die, it's all good.'

'Ha, she barely had enough gold for one night here. Speaking of before they die, though … did you hear who passed through yesterday?'

'No?'

'Only Sekobi the Trickster.'

'Get away.'

'It's true! Old Kezman was on the gate, recognised him straight away.'

'So he's back. For one last glory run, d'you think?'

'Who knows. I thought he'd gone for good. Ha, next we'll be having Longholm the Warrior back. And Moshab, and Marsali Quil…'

'Well, that would be impressive, given they're all dead last I heard … but who knows…' And they laughed, and called in Ganhaw to be searched.

A hand was placed on Azra's shoulder. Instinctively, she clenched her fists, but before she could disappear a familiar voice spoke.

'I told you to be more alert.'

She relaxed when she saw Sekobi. 'Come with me,' he said. 'Keep a bit of a distance, though.'

'I thought the Rule of One was only for inside the Warren?' Azra asked.

'It is,' the trickster replied. 'But best not to raise any unnecessary attention.' He set off, throwing over his shoulder: 'Try not to disappear along the way.'

The Citadel was unlike anywhere Azra had seen before. It had wide, clean streets, with arrays of inns, armourers, shops offering all kinds of magical equipment, all promising that they alone would ensure success in the Warren. Everywhere there were adventurers – mostly men or women, but also elves, some dwarves, here and there a hybrid creature that Azra could not determine, but didn't want to look at for too long.

Sekobi weaved through the streets, and while he kept a low profile he seemed somehow more upright here, his shoulders wider, his head more aloft. Azra supposed that at least he wasn't wanted for any crimes here. That she knew of, anyway.

They had come to an avenue with particularly extravagant shopfronts. She noted the prices were far higher here than shops they had passed by before – even though they seemed to be for much the same things. Looking up, she could see they had got closer to the palace.

She followed Sekobi into a large building. Inside, it was instantly quieter and cooler: a marble atrium, with large iron doors set into the walls on all sides. Sekobi waited for Azra to join him. The atrium was empty but for an elderly clerk sat at a desk behind a metal grille. He looked up, and simply nodded: 'Master Sekobi.'

Sekobi walked purposefully to one of the doors, indiscernible from the others, and inserted a key to open it. This led to a long corridor, lit only by shafts of light from high up in the ceiling. They walked down it, until Sekobi abruptly stopped. Here was another door: thick set, enforced with metal bands and a formidable lock in the centre. With a different key, Sekobi twisted the lock, muttering something indistinct under his breath. There was a sudden cold breeze, gone as soon as it was there, and the door heaved open. Sekobi stepped back for Azra to see inside.

Azra peered forward and took a sharp breath.

The room before her was piled high with riches. Gold coins, gemstones, crowns, rings and the finest silk and cloths, overloading the tables and shelves they sat on.

Sekobi entered, holding his hands out and sighing gently. He looked over at Azra. 'You see, once, I was a king here.'

And for a moment, Azra wondered if Sekobi was thinking about staying there, and becoming the great adventurer again, becoming the trickster king of the Warren. But, just as quickly, the moment disappeared from his face.

'It all means nothing,' he said, and for the first time since meeting him, Azra noted he sounded genuinely sad. 'It's all worthless.' And he kicked a pile of gold as if it were loose shingle on a beach, before beginning to rummage in a chest.

Azra felt gripped by an intense feeling in her stomach. So much gold. And the memory of Vane's warnings – 'Do not get distracted by treasure hunting, friends, for our prize is far greater' – fought with her instincts to pocket at least some of Sekobi's winnings. Her thoughts were interrupted by the trickster, who had fished out a sheet of parchment and black chalk.

'Draw me the map,' he said. 'The map to the meeting point.'

Azra took up the chalk and sketched, with a speed that Sekobi was clearly not expecting, the lines and links of the passages in the Warren she would have to negotiate before they met again. She had spent a long time in the house committing it to memory, sat next to Sylvindor relating endless stories of his time in the tree village.

'Very good,' said Sekobi, nodding. He scooped up the paper and, with a short movement of his fingers, it caught alight in a red flame and disintegrated. 'I can see why Vane chose you. Less so the elf, but we'll see I suppose.'

Then he turned back to the chest.

'If you want a weapon, take one,' he said, over his shoulder. 'No doubt it will serve you better than whatever Quil passed off to you as a sword. For me, I prefer this...'

He turned around with a flourish, holding a weapon – a long shank with a curved end, menacingly sharp and emitting a faint glow.

'This kind of falx is illegal in the outside world,' Sekobi said. 'Too deadly for mere mortals. Too deadly for most in the Warren too.'

'Too deadly for a dragon?' asked Azra.

Sekobi smiled his crooked smile. 'We shall see...'

6

At the Eastern Door

Azra spent the night in one of the cheaper hotels, which Sekobi had passed her some gold to pay for. He had gone his own way, apparently to some lodgings he owned from back in his time in Skala that were now looked after by a 'friend'. While his accommodation was far grander and undoubtedly more comfortable, he had reminded her of the need to not be seen too much together, so it was a rough mattress for her.

This didn't matter too much to Azra, for whom any kind of bed was a comfort she was not often used to. However, she struggled to sleep, going over and over in her head the plans, and considering all the things that could go wrong. She had no idea if Quil and Sylvindor were even in Skala – those two were to make brief contact with each other and then enter the Warren separately. Vane was to arrange for transport of the gold from the outside. She would be waiting within the caves on the other side of the alleged magic door.

Yes, there was a lot that could go wrong. But despite this, Azra was in no doubt she had made the right decision. She had already learned much from her new acquaintances. And what life did she have to return to, anyway? Not anywhere with a hotel bed, that's for sure – cheap or not.

She worried about Sylvindor, though. His enthusiasm betrayed an upbringing without hardship. He seemed too quick to trust, too keen to show his abilities, and despite their many conversations over the past few days he had never disclosed why he had been banished from his homeland. Nor did he betray any bitterness or regret from this. He was unlike anyone Azra had ever met – although, as she reminded herself, she hadn't met many people, and very few, perhaps none, who showed any real friendliness towards her.

In the morning, she used more of the gold to buy some provisions, which she filled her backpack with.

'Planning on a long trip?' asked the storekeeper, raising an eyebrow. 'If it's your first time, lass, I'd be careful. Don't want to be spending more than a day or so down there until you get your feet. Got to acclimatise, see? The air is different down there.'

'I'm sure I'll be fine,' she replied, not looking back at him.

The storekeeper laughed. 'Oh, do you know how many times I've heard that before?' Then he leaned over the counter towards Azra. 'And do you know what they all say when they come back?'

There was a pause. Azra lifted her head from her pack, and raised an eyebrow, knowing full well what he would say next.

'Nothing,' he hissed. ''Cos they're all *dead*!'

'I appreciate your concern,' said Azra, sarcastically. And then, just to annoy the storekeeper, she clenched her fists and in an instant was outside the shop. Hearing him stutter an exclamation about cursed magic users amused her, and she weaved her way through the street towards the Eastern Door.

Sekobi, she knew, had set off earlier in the morning, and was aiming to enter the Northern Door. This was, by reputation, a more difficult entrance to the Warren, and it would raise no suspicion that an experienced adventurer would use it. The Eastern Door, meanwhile, was the largest, and the typical starting point for most embarking on their descent into the caves. Quil and Sylvindor would both use the Western Door – Quil had been keen to enter as near to the elf as possible, because (she had muttered to Azra one night) she felt he needed the most guarding. 'His sword is quick alright,' she had said, 'but he's clearly trained like a noble, and nobles expect their enemies to be in front of them, going through the traditional motions. Nobody stands in front of you in the Warren. Especially not when you first get in.'

This point had been drilled into them. Because of the dangers of the lower levels, it was not unknown for less honourable visitors to hide inside the entrances, and attack newcomers before they could adjust to the darkness. 'From the moment you're inside,' Quil had said, as she taught Azra how to use her sword, 'every moment is one in which your life could be taken. Every shadow is an enemy, every sound is a threat.'

'Is that how you won so much in the Warren?' Sylvindor had asked. 'Being the most alert?'

'You don't win,' Quil had replied. 'You just stay alive.'

To her relief, Azra did not have to queue again for the Eastern Door. She rounded a corner and found a square, its sides lined with market stalls against the white buildings, all advertising 'last minute' equipment or 'welcome out' hospitality. In the middle of the square was a raised stone platform, surrounded by tall banners of black and silver. Several guards were standing around on top of it, along with some wooden contraptions, tables and chests; and behind it, two burly looking men, possibly half-giants Azra thought, were playing some form of board game. Set into the platform was a huge wooden trapdoor, flat against the ground.

As Azra took a step on to the platform the nearest guard held up his hand, shouting 'Halt!' sharply. Another guard lowered his spear towards her. 'Not one step further!'

She stopped, and her heart sped up a little. Did they know about the plan already? Had Sekobi given the game away? Were the others found out...?

But the guards now turned back to the centre of the platform, and one had his head bent towards it.

'Yeah, that was definitely a knock that time.'

'Nah, it came from the inn. Probably a door slamming somewhere.'

They listened again. Above the noise of the square, Azra was sure she heard a faint tapping sound.

The guard straightened up. 'We're going to have to open it,' he said, and another guard sighed.

The guard who had spoken to Azra ordered her off the platform. She did so, watching as the guards now formed a well-rehearsed circle around the trapdoor, spears pointing towards it. The two half-giants paused their game and began to heave a rope on a pulley system. Slowly, the door creaked, and lifted from the ground. The guards remained still, tensed, waiting to see what was there. With a final pull, the mechanism eased and the trapdoor swung upwards. The guards tentatively peered forward, and then one leaned in.

'It's alright, fella, here you are,' he said. Then, to the other guards, he said: 'Looks safe, lads.'

Another guard helped him reach down and pull someone out from inside. They dragged him to one side of the platform, then signalled the half-giants to drop the rope. The trapdoor fell with an immense crash.

Azra could now see that the figure was an adventurer, but he looked in a really bad way. The first guard patted him on the back as he lay, gasping for air and clearly blinded by the morning sun.

'Alright now, fella,' he said again. 'You made it out. Hope you got something good for all that. Now, where's your permit, son?'

The adventurer was half-dead, Azra thought, and seemed in no state to answer. Another guard poked him. 'He's got it there in his hand, give me a second...' and he retrieved a scrap of parchment. 'Good to have this,' he said, patting the adventurer's head. 'Otherwise, we have to send you back down.'

Permit secured, the first guard was keen for him to move on. 'Get yourself to that stall over there, son, he'll give you some drink on credit. Mind you, you'll need to pay him eventually. Now get away from the entrance, we need to keep this place clean and clear.'

Azra watched as the adventurer, who seemed to not quite know where he was, crawled away. Several market sellers instantly started shouting at him to come over and buy their healing potions.

Azra's gaze was interrupted by one of the guards. 'Hey, you,' he said. 'Were you coming in?'

Azra turned back to her goal. She nodded, and stepped up to the platform.

'First time?' asked the guard. Azra was getting increasingly annoyed with this question, but nodded all the same.

'Even after seeing him?' asked another guard, motioning towards the adventurer, who by this time seemed to have stopped crawling, or moving at all.

Azra nodded again. 'Just let me in,' she said.

'Hold your horses, young 'un,' replied the first guard. 'There's the small matter of the entrance fee. You need a permit.'

'I have the fee here,' Azra said, taking out the pouch from her belt.

'Well, aren't you prepared,' replied the guard. He pointed to one of the tables. 'Then there are the extras. We don't *need* to know who you are, but if you want your entry noted for official records, you do it there. Only two gold pieces, and worth it if you want bragging rights in the tavern.'

'She's not old enough to brag in a tavern,' said one of the other guards, laughing.

The first guard continued: 'If you want to leave a last will and testament, or a message to your loved ones, we can ensure they receive it after the length of time you decree without re-emerging. That's a flat rate for the first three days, but it goes up after that to a maximum of one year. We only retain documents, with the exception of regular-sized rings and bracelets, for an increased fee. Understand?'

'I just want to go in,' Azra said. But the guard hadn't finished. He clearly had a set speech to finish.

'Any damage sustained while in the Warren is the sole responsibility of the entrant, and the Baron Kaveshvill will make no attempt to retrieve your body, dead or alive, from inside the Warren once you have passed through the door. Understand?' he asked again.

Azra was getting impatient. 'Why would he do that anyway?' she said, almost to herself.

'Lots of rich folk don't like losing their sons and daughters. They can come here offering a lot of gold for us to go down there and search for them. Ha! Not our job, is it? Hire someone from the taverns, pay their king's ransom...'

'I don't have any parents, and I'm not rich,' snapped Azra, irritated. 'Can I go in now?'

The guard folded his arms. 'Are you rich enough for the entrance fee?'

Azra handed over the last of the gold that Sekobi had given to her. The guard emptied the leather pouch on to the table, and quickly counted it up.

'It's all here,' he said to the others, then nodded at the half-giants. They began to heave again, and the rest of the guards assembled in their circle once more, spears pointing forward.

'You want to come out, you bang on the door. Bang hard, and have your permit ready or you'll need to pay to get out,' the guard warned. 'Oh, and watch for anyone hiding by the stairs ... that's all the free advice you're getting.'

The door swung upwards again, and Azra stepped forward. In front of her was a stone staircase, leading downwards into what seemed to be pitch black. There was a funny smell drifting out from the dark, a dank, sweaty smell that was quite unlike anything she'd encountered before.

Taking one last look at the square around her, and the blue sky above her, Azra nodded to the guard, checked the sword at her belt and the pack on her shoulders, and headed down.

7

Descent into darkness

Azra had got halfway down the stone steps when the trapdoor slammed above her, and the light of the sun was banished for the foreseeable future. She breathed in, and was caught by a musty, rotting smell that seemed to surround her. *Perhaps this is what death smells like*, she thought. And her hands began to warm, but not itch.

She was caught up in this thought as she reached the bottom of the steps, feeling her way as her eyes attempted to adjust to the darkness. There were faint flickers of torchlight far off, and here and there she began to make out the edge of a wall, the arch of a passageway. But it was still too dark to move. She gulped, and remembered something Quil had said.

'Don't descend too quickly...'

At this thought, something sharp and cold was pressed against the back of her neck.

'I've been waiting for you.' She heard the voice of the warrior at the gate, Ganhaw. 'Silly child, coming to play a grown up's game. Now I'll be taking your gold, and your head...'

Of all the idiotic things ... Azra was furious with herself. She had made the mistake Quil and Sekobi had warned her of time and time again. And now she had a sword up against her.

But then she felt the warmth in her hands again, and rather than panic, she sighed and relaxed her shoulders.

'Should have taken up the tavern work, darling...' Ganhaw was saying. But he got no further.

In an instant, Azra was behind him, a good few feet in the air, and in one movement she drew her sword and plunged it into Ganhaw's unprotected back.

The man fell to his knees, choking and spluttering. Azra wondered whether to stab him again. But at that point, she became aware of another figure alongside her. The figure approached Ganhaw, and calmly pushed him to the floor, where he shook for a moment, then lay still. Then the figure turned to Azra.

'I would applaud your first kill, had it not been in such foolish circumstances,' Sekobi said.

Azra breathed deeply, then narrowed her eyes. 'Have you been waiting there all this time?'

Sekobi shrugged. 'At Quil's request. Apparently, this plan has enough risks without anyone getting killed too early.'

'I was *fine*,' Azra said, defiantly.

'Indeed. Then I will leave you to get to the staircase. Try and stay out of trouble. And try not to vanish too much. Not on the early levels.'

'Why?'

'Because the shadows can be … unreliable.'

And with that, he was gone.

Azra felt a little hurt at Sekobi's chiding. It was best to not hang around the entrance for too long, though. Stopping only to loot Ganhaw's backpack of its gold, she moved on.

She had, of course, been well-briefed on what to expect, but what neither Quil nor Sekobi had mentioned was that the first level of the Warren was surprisingly noisy. Despite the darkness of the passageways, lit only from sparse lanterns here and there, or the odd glowing waterfall, spilling down the sides of the wall – 'don't drink from those,' Quil had said, 'Nobody wants to be seeing clouds in a dungeon' – she found herself very much aware of the other adventurers pacing the tunnels. Sometimes it was the noise of blades clashing in anger, sometimes a scream of fear, sometimes a call to warn others. 'Changeling!' one shout came from somewhere behind Azra. 'Watch for the…' The voice had stopped suddenly, and Azra assumed that the changeling had not taken well to being identified.

'Why do people help each other like that?' Sylvindor had asked back at the house. 'I thought that was against the Rule of One?'

'And what would you do in your last moment in this world?' Sekobi had replied. 'When all is lost, sword at your throat, no riches for you, likely nobody to find your body even ... perhaps you would die silently, perhaps you would use that moment for one last gift to the world you're leaving.'

'That's one way of looking at it,' Quil had remarked from the other side of the room. 'It's more simple, though. Some adventurers think you have to fight fair. And if they see something...' and she fixed a look on Sekobi. '...trickster-like, something to disadvantage the game, then, well, they'll shout.'

The memories of their time in the house allowed Azra to refocus, and she found her bearings quickly. She had spent time on her journey to Skala memorising the maps of the first few levels and the path she needed to take. She didn't want to waste time and put herself at risk by stopping to look at the map itself. Especially now she had found out how dangerous a loss of attention could be, even for a second.

Once her initial nerves settled, and the strangeness of the underground world became more familiar, she realised that the first level was not all that different from any city or town. Instead of guards and townsfolk, down every passageway and past every opening there was usually some kind of adventurer stalking, looking for their next challenger. And just as Azra had learned to avoid guards and townsfolk without having to vanish at all, she found the same tricks worked in the Warren too. Moving with purpose, staying out of any natural eye-line, and using the full height of the area – working through gutters where she found them, climbing up ledges, using old lantern hangings and chains lodged in the ceiling to stealthily make her way past any potential adversaries.

The easiest way, of course, was to simply turn the adventurers on themselves. If she became aware of two near each other, sending a rock or scrap of metal singing across the passageway would soon alert them to each other's presence, and in the fight that followed she could easily slip by undetected. Every so often she was aware of things that were not human – sometimes they were dead at the hands of a previous adventurer, and sometimes they were very much alive, hunting the next unwary explorer.

Azra kept clear of all of them. Keeping clear of people was what she did best. She had done it most of her life, and certainly back in her home village nobody would be pleased to see her.

She didn't like to talk about her village, and was grateful that the closest anyone had come to questioning her on where she came from was Quil, who had briefly asked her if she had parents. When Azra said no, Quil simply nodded. 'Everyone leaves you in the end,' she had said, weighing her sword in her had. 'You'll see the benefits of this when it's time.' And then they had continued to spar.

In fact, all of them had steered well away from discussing Vane's descriptions of them, almost as much as Quil and Sekobi steered clear of each other. Only Sylvindor talked about Haemir, the great elven forest he once called home, though never what led him to leave it. For the trust they must have in each other for the plan to succeed, Azra thought, they seemed to be focused only on their skills in combat and magic.

She had been concerned that, despite Quil's training and Sekobi's insights, she lacked the obvious skills the others had. Now she was in the Warren, she saw that her ability to keep out of the way was a decided advantage in staying alive, at least for this level. She used her memory of the maps and her stealth to navigate the Warren, and through that seemed quite invisible.

The only time she broke her focus was to pocket the gold or supplies left on any of the bodies she passed.

At one point, as she paused to eat some stale bread she had found from just such a source, she thought that knowing how her abilities helped here would have been useful earlier in the house.

'Is there anything else you can do?' Sekobi had asked her once.

'What do you mean?' Azra asked.

'I mean, vanishing ... that's a great trick. Rare, you know. But is it your only one?'

Azra had confessed she'd never been asked about that before, and would have to think about it. She had gone to move past him, but Sekobi caught her by the arms, rolling his eyes.

'Listen, people don't like magic, right? People don't trust it. But they panic at vanishers. Down in the Warren, if someone sees you, they'll spread the word. Vanisher in the tunnels!'

And he raised his arms for dramatic effect.

'And then it's harder to pull off the trick, see?'

'It's not a trick,' Azra protested. 'It's just something I ... do.'

'No,' Sekobi said, bringing his face close to hers. 'It's something you *are*.'

Azra bristled a little. She met his eyes with hers. 'Then it's something *you* are too.'

Sekobi didn't move for a moment, as if he were noticing something, even though his face remained set on Azra. Then he smiled his strange lop-sided smile.

'No. I'm a lot of things, but not a vanisher.'

He straightened up. 'Listen. In the Warren, magic is stronger. You'll be able to go further, quicker. But you need to watch the shadows. Things aren't always as they seem down there.'

'I'm getting that impression.'

Sekobi folded his arms. 'Well, I see you've answered my question. Best get back to Quil's sword lessons.'

Vanisher

Azra returned a half-smile, and went to go.

'But,' Sekobi grabbed her arm again. 'I'll have my money back first.'

Azra glared, and from her pocket she produced the pouch that she had relieved from Sekobi's belt only a few moments ago. Placing it on the table, she said: 'It's not a trick.'

'No,' Sekobi said. 'But effective.'

He picked up the pouch and weighed it. 'So you are a thief. Well, I'm sure I can show you some... tricks... to help with that.'

8

The long passage

In the constant dark of the Warren's maze-like tunnels, there was no day and night. It was a long time before Azra reached the stairway which led down to the second level, and she was feeling heavy with tiredness. She had already seen some adventurers suffering from lack of sleep – desperately trying to find their way to the exit, with bloodshot eyes and unbalanced strides. This, Azra reflected, was not a good position to be in.

Nevertheless, she was still wary enough to hold back at the sight of the stairs and check to see if anyone was loitering, waiting to jump on the unsuspecting explorer.

It didn't take long to see not one, but two figures at the top of the stairway. Creeping through the shadows, Azra listened to their conversation.

'I say we move on,' said the first, a tall woman with an unkind tone. 'With you at the bottom of the stairs and me at the top, we've easily taken enough gold to see us right for a few weeks outside.'

The other, a young man, was pouring a pouch of gold into a larger knapsack.

'We can't move out together, people will see we've been working together,' he said.

The woman scowled. 'True. I don't want my neck snapped by the Baron.'

'Well, look, I'll keep hold of the gold and we can meet at Stetler's Tavern later.'

'Are you joking?' scoffed the woman. 'You think I'd let you walk out with all the takings? Divide it up. Now.'

'It's too dark to divide it up properly,' replied the man.

'Then do a rough split now and we can count it properly at the tavern.'

'I don't ... oh, fine. Pass me your pack, and keep a watch out.'

The man turned away from the woman, who readied her sword. Her eyes by now well-accustomed to the gloom, Azra could see that the man was tipping gold into the two knapsacks, but was clearly not dividing it equally.

'Keep your eyes peeled,' he said over his shoulder to the woman. 'Wouldn't want anyone to know we've broken the Rule of One.'

The woman, still with her sword drawn, moved so she stood over him. 'Oh, but you see, we're not breaking it.'

'What do you mean?' asked the man, focused on ensuring he got the larger share of the gold. Then he stopped and his face changed. 'Wait...'

It was too late. The woman brought her sword down on to his undefended back, and in a moment he had slumped to the floor. The woman laughed a little to herself, scooped up the treasure, and made her way off down the passage.

It seems like the Rule of One always wins in the end, thought Azra to herself.

She took the opportunity to descend the stairs, keeping a sharp lookout for any lurking enemies, but assuming the previous two would have kept the way clear for now. She needed to find somewhere to sleep.

These stairs, she knew from Quil and Sekobi's accounts, were a less well-known route to the second level. They took her to a narrow passageway which she quickly moved out of, into a small open square. Two doorways led into what seemed like rooms either side of her, and ahead there was what seemed to be a longer corridor stretching out into the dark. This certainly matched what the map had said. The second level would be less populated than the first, but Azra would also have to consult her map more. There was a short cut to the next stairway, where they were planning to meet up.

Not wanting to be out in the open space by the stairs too long, she moved towards the room on her left. It could be a good place to rest, but also a good place to walk into a trap. She stopped at the entrance and cautiously raised her arm. Concentrating, she felt her hand warming, and this time small streaks of heat fled from her shoulder down to her hand. As she felt the streaks move into her fingers, she flicked her thumb up, then gasped a little. A small flame had appeared, hovering above her hand.

It seemed like Sekobi's tricks were worth something after all – even if she had struggled to do it this easily back at the house.

In fact, as she cast her flame across the room to check it was empty of traps or enemies, she found that she was already feeling less tired. Instead, a strange sort of energy had taken up inside her. Unsure at first, she then remembered Sekobi's claim that the magic got stronger the lower the Warren went.

Well, this must be what it feels like to be magical, Azra thought to herself.

Instead of resting, and having searched briefly for any treasure, she decided to press on. Ahead of her was the long passageway which she would need to go through. It was wide compared to some of the walkways in the level above, but offered very little in the way of hiding places, especially if anyone had a torch.

Perhaps, Azra thought, perhaps she could try vanishing. The way seemed clear, and if she got far enough then she wouldn't have to worry about being caught in the open by anyone coming the other way. True, she may not be able to go the whole way, as she had never vanished that far in one go. But at least it would make the journey safer for part of it.

Not wanting to loiter anymore, Azra charged her hands up. In the blink of an eye, she moved – not halfway down the passageway, as she had expected, but right to the end, slamming uncomfortably into the wall. Dazed from the impact, she staggered slightly to the side, turning a corner – and almost walking straight into a tall man.

She only saw that his face was blood-smeared, and he had a crazed look behind a thick beard of sweat and cobwebs. For a single moment, he looked caught by surprise at the small girl in front of him. The very next moment, he had drawn a huge, double-handed sword from behind his back and swung it straight at her.

Azra dodged the blow, and while her instinct was to vanish again, she instead drew her sword and kept in mind Quil's training. 'Use their strength against them,' she had said. The warrior swung again, and again Azra hopped away, feeling the rush of air from the blade glance across her face. She sized up her opponent. There was no way she could win in a straight fight here. As he brought his sword crashing down towards her, she rolled to the side, bumping into the hard wall. The knock took the wind out of her, and any chance to counterattack was lost. Instead, with her on the floor, he moved in for the kill.

Forget this, Azra thought. As the blade came towards her, she rolled again – this time further into the shadows where two walls met. She should have been caught by the sword – but when the warrior drew his weapon back, expecting to see blood, he realised he had missed again.

'There's nowhere to run now!' he cried, and stabbed furiously into the dark corner. But then: 'Hey, what's this? Where have you gone?'

He stepped forward, slashing fruitlessly in the dark. 'Where's she gone?' he snarled, looking all around him. A noise, further down the hall, caught his attention. 'Running again, are you? I'll make you pay!'

He charged off. Resting above on a small protrusion, Azra breathed. *That was a close one*, she thought, nursing her head from where she had accidentally struck it against the stone above.

She hopped down, quickly consulting her map. At that point, her attention was caught by a movement – this time from the shadows across the way.

She folded the map away, and walked towards it, irritated. 'Still watching me, Sekobi? I've told you I can look after myself.'

There was another movement in the darkness, a shuffling and something that could have been a laugh.

Azra defiantly made straight for it. 'Look, I've already said...'

The shadow was suddenly illuminated by a bright light, blinding her for a moment before her eyes grew accustomed and she saw before her, not Sekobi, but a hideous lizard face, its mouth open with rows of razor sharp teeth and a wicked tongue stretching out for her neck, while two claws grabbed her arms and dug in.

Azra was caught completely by surprise, but her instincts were also quick to engage. Realising that struggling against the lizardman's hold was futile, she instead threw her legs up, landing a kick to its groin while also flipping herself backwards, away from the strangling tongue. Almost fully rotated, she aimed another kick to the lizardman's jaw, feeling her boot crack a number of teeth. The creature howled, and released its grip. Azra fell back to the floor, twisting to avoid landing on her head. She had only a moment before the lizardman leapt for her, but in that time she drew her sword and swung, impaling the creature in mid-air.

It fell to the floor, and Azra lay, breathing heavily. What Sekobi had said was true. The shadows could be unreliable.

9

A reunion

Azra saw many strange creatures, and equally strange adventurers, as she passed through the second level. But just as in the first level, she was keen to keep out of their way. The route drawn on her map took her through a back route, one which only the experience of Quil and Sekobi could have negotiated, through small chambers and hidden corridors that most of the Warren's inhabitants would never find.

It was harder going, as more than once she took a wrong turn and had to create light to view the map again. Each time, she risked being seen, or drawing the attention of any passing creature. But while this made her progress slower, and she strained to keep her concentration and nerves, the same energy she had felt at the stairs remained. It was ... exciting.

Eventually she found her way to the third level, a half-concealed spiral staircase in the corner of a complex of rooms. Satisfied there was nobody about, she climbed downwards, keeping her sword poised and a flame in front of her, to avoid mis-stepping and tumbling down the rest of the stairs.

The way down was longer than she expected, but she took her time, stopping every so often to listen for any sound of another person either below or above her. She could feel the atmosphere of the Warren changing around her, and the energy growing.

At last, she made out an archway leading out to the third level. She was stepping quietly, but realised that the light from the flame at her hand would give away her presence to anybody waiting below. She paused, thought, then smiled to herself. Bringing her hand into a clenched fist, she then swung her arm forward – and the flame leapt out of her grasp and out through the archway, like a single fiery arrow.

She followed it, hoping it would surprise or blind any potential enemies. Almost immediately, she saw a blade jabbing towards her throat. But Azra was ready, her own sword already moving to repel the attack. Before she could react further, though, she heard a familiar voice.

'Clearly my training has paid off.'

She took note of her surroundings. It was a small chamber, with two burning torches providing light and shadows in equal measure. Standing over two or three bodies, Quil put her broadsword to the floor and rested on the hilt. She smiled.

'Nice trick with the fireworks as well. Novel, certainly,' she said.

Azra smiled back and nodded.

'Well, I see you made it in one piece,' Quil continued. 'Even if you are a bit late. Come on, we're through here.'

'Did—did everyone make it?' she asked.

'Sylvindor is alive, if that's what you mean. A good job he's as quick with the sword as he is his step, but he made it.'

'And Sekobi?'

Quil was already moving on. 'Unfortunately, yes...' she muttered.

There was a series of smaller chambers, before Quil led her into a room off to one side. It was low-ceilinged, but warm from a brazier in the middle of some rubble. Sekobi was sat cross-legged in one corner, while Sylvindor had already bounded up to Azra the moment she entered.

He gave her a huge, and quite unexpected, hug.

'It's so good to see you!' he said.

'Er ... yeah, yes. You too, Syl.' Azra was not used to being hugged. Quil found this amusing, and she leaned towards the fire and scooped up some cooked meat.

'Here,' she said. 'Have some food. We'll rest up here for a while before moving out.'

Azra looked at the meat. 'What is it?'

'Best not to ask,' Quil replied. 'There's water in that flask. Be sure to drink it. There are fresher streams nearby. I'm not having any tunnel madness while we're here.'

Azra sat down in the only space available, at the far corner opposite Sekobi.

'Cosy, isn't it?' he said, chewing on something. 'Probably a good thing that giant couldn't come along, all things considered.'

Azra nodded, and started to eat. The charred taste from the brazier did its best to mask whatever it was she was ingesting. She didn't mind. She hadn't quite realised how hungry she was.

'Have you had many adventures?' Sylvindor hissed at her, keenly. 'I've taken at least three orcs in one hour alone.'

'The stories can wait,' said Quil, standing at the doorway and checking outside. 'We'll all need to get some sleep. I'll take first watch.'

'Will you?' Sekobi raised an eyebrow and swallowed. 'Hardly wise, Marsali Quil. What if the watch is reminded of the Rule of One, while the rest of us sleep?'

Quil gave him a disdainful look. 'I hardly think we need worry about that,' she said. 'We all know why we're here.'

Sekobi shook his head, calmly. 'Two on watch. Two sleep. We'll change when the log burns down.'

Quil considered. 'Agreed.'

Sekobi stretched. 'You and the elf seem to have had the most … excitement on the way down. Azra and I will take first watch.'

Quil didn't reply, but nodded, as if she was weighing up the advantages of Sekobi's suggestion and deciding it was worth following, for now.

Azra watched as Quil sat down, resting against the stone wall with her pack against her head, and her sword firmly between her two hands. Sylvindor, also watching, attempted to get into the same position, though found it more difficult as a large pile of rocks and broken pottery was behind him. Eventually, he gave up, and lay flat on the ground. 'Just like back on the streets!' he murmured, and closed his eyes.

Azra finished her meal, washing down the dirty meat with Quil's water. Then she sat. This was the first time, she realised, she had been this still since entering the Warren. After a short while, she began to wonder what on earth she was meant to do for all the time she was on 'watch'.

Apart from the small fire, all was dark, and for once there was hardly any noise from the passages and tunnels beyond them. The occasional shriek, the odd clang, but they were well hidden here, and Azra found herself staring at the strange patterns on the walls around them, the remains of what looked like pillars, and then to the fire in the middle of the room. For a while, she was lost in aimless thoughts.

'I have the sense you're enjoying yourself here,' Sekobi said, his voice somehow melding with the shadows.

'I've not thought about it,' Azra replied.

'You don't need to think about it,' Sekobi replied. 'You feel it.'

Azra looked across at him. 'I do feel ... stronger. Like you said. The ... magic.'

'Indeed.'

The flames in the brazier leapt and danced, lighting up Sekobi's face across from her in ever-shifting ways. Only his eyes remained dark, fixed upon Azra.

'I couldn't help but notice,' he said, softly, 'you seemed awfully ... calm... after your first kill.'

Azra said nothing. The words instinctively brought back a memory. In the dark, the man in front of her, the blade in her hand.

She shrugged. 'It happened so quickly.'

'Yes.' Sekobi's eyes didn't move. 'An instinctive move.'

Azra's mind was replaying the scene, even though she had no wish for it to. The man, his snarling face, the blade, her rage...

'I was remembering what I'd been taught,' she said, aware that she said it slightly fiercely.

'Perhaps,' Sekobi said. 'I would say it was more instinctive. A thief's instincts, perhaps.'

Thief! The burning in her hands, the blade in her hands, the man bringing his fists towards her as he shouted again: *thief!*

'Or the instincts of someone else. Someone who has, perhaps, killed before.'

Azra's mind was far away. The man on the floor, dead. The cold night wind tugging her guilt away. The village around her still, the man's shouting drowned by the tavern nearby. The burning in her hands.

Sekobi's mouth twisted into a smile. 'Not just a thief, then. A murderer too.'

Azra felt herself return to reality, the warmth of the brazier's fire and the discomfort of the Warren's ground. She looked back at Sekobi, and for no reason she knew, she felt her throat tighten slightly.

'I didn't ask for *any* of this,' she said.

'No, we never ask for it.' Sekobi folded his arms and took in a long, deep breath. 'Not the first time, anyway.'

10

Moshab

Azra was awoken from a dreamless sleep by a sharp kick.

'Enough rest for now,' said Quil. 'We need to move.'

Sylvindor was exercising, or trying to exercise in the cramped room, while Sekobi was adjusting his pack.

'I suppose we must be careful of anyone now,' the elf said. 'Well, more than usual I mean.'

'We must not be seen together,' Sekobi said, checking the edge of his falx. 'No witnesses.'

'I'm sure that won't be an issue,' said Quil, hauling her pack on to her back. 'If we take the narrow route from here, we'll soon meet Moshab.'

'Who's Moshab?' asked Sylvindor.

'I thought we were alone?' asked Azra, at exactly the same time.

Sekobi chuckled. 'Let's just say he's a ... landmark of sorts.'

'Beyond Moshab we'll be unlikely to see any more humans,' said Quil. 'Or elves.'

Azra got to her feet. She wondered if she should also check her stuff, but as her pack was untouched since she had got there, and she had slept with her sword by her side, there was nothing to ready. She had learned to make quick exits over the years. She loitered uselessly while Sylvindor finished whatever it was he was doing, and they set off, walking in a line with Quil at the front.

Sylvindor turned to Azra. 'Did you sleep okay? I thought I heard you talking in your...'

'Ssh!' snapped Quil. 'We travel in silence. Wait until the next stop for your pleasantries.'

Sylvindor looked a little stunned, as Quil's tone was harsh, and he had simply forgotten where they were for the moment.

Quil, realising she had hurt his feelings, gave him an awkward pat on the shoulder. 'We need you alert, young man. Er, elf.'

'Man-elf,' muttered Sekobi, for no reason.

Sylvindor shot him a glare. 'I'm not a...'

Sekobi raised his finger to his lips, with a lop-sided smile that was not entirely friendly. 'Ssh,' he said, and raised an eyebrow.

They soon fell into a rhythm, following Quil's path. Azra, at the back of the group, kept her eyes behind them, every so often tugging on Sekobi's arm to indicate a noise or a movement from somewhere in the far shadows, at which point they would pause, remain still, until Sekobi motioned to move on.

Azra's view of Quil was more difficult, as the passageways were even darker on this level, but she remained impressed at how both the veteran adventurers continuously scanned their surroundings, sometimes for enemies, sometimes for traps, sometimes for memories of previous experiences down there. At one point, they reached two doorways, and Quil turned to Sekobi, who silently pointed to the one on the right. Another time, Quil made for a small room off the main passage, and Sekobi coughed. But Quil shook her head, and continued. Inside, there was a row of statues against the wall – strange, not-quite human-looking statues which were too old and worn to show what they may have once been. With no hesitation, Quil took hold of one and lifted it, moving it to one side and revealing a passageway behind it.

Sekobi let out a quiet, impressed laugh.

Their knowledge of hidden routes meant they were only dimly aware of other inhabitants from vague noises. Indeed, apart from a mishap with what might have been an orc – Quil dispatched it quickly and silently – these reputedly more dangerous levels were far emptier than the higher levels. After a while, Azra noticed Quil begin to visibly relax her shoulders a little, and Sekobi turned back to Azra and whispered: 'Very quiet here today.'

The walls around them had widened out, forming a kind of plaza, with the vaulted ceiling high above and a range of doorways leading off. In the middle was a large metal post, and hanging high above was a cage.

Sekobi stood before the cage and did something like a salute. 'Good to see you again, my friend,' he said.

Azra looked up. In the cage was a corpse, long rotted to the bones, with torn rags of what was once armour. The only thing left on it was a pair of bright green boots, caught on the cage bars.

'Moshab?' she asked.

Quil stood behind her. 'That was his name, yes. The finest adventurer to walk the Warren. Well, until he was overtaken by two others.'

'What happened to him?' Sylvindor asked, and he looked troubled by something. His bright eyes watched this way and that way, and he certainly didn't seem to want to look at the skeleton above them.

'Moshab? Old Moshi? Mosser?' Sekobi replied. 'He had the run of this level. He came up with an idea, see, once he had taken his share of fighting in the levels above. Rather than face the swarms of kobolds and goblins down here, he traded with them. You know – made friends, like.'

'Is that, you know ... in the rules?' queried Azra.

'He would say so,' Sekobi said. 'It was up for interpretation, though. I'm not sure the Baron would have seen it that way.'

'I don't like it here,' murmured Sylvindor. 'We should move on.'

'What happened to him, though?' asked Azra.

Sekobi shrugged. 'You can see what happened to him. I imagine the goblins weren't as up for trading as he'd first thought.'

Quil sighed. 'Nobody knows. But he's been a landmark since he got up there.'

'A landmark for what?'

'For the point of no return,' she said, grimly. 'From here, it all gets a lot tougher…'

'We should really move,' said Sylvindor, who was by now already further away from the rest of the group, trying to encourage them towards one of the exits.

'Yes, let's get going,' Quil agreed, and pointed to one of the doorways. 'The way is through there.'

'The way to what?' asked Azra, half to herself as she continued to look up at Moshab.

'To hell,' Sekobi patted her on the shoulder to follow. 'So long, big Mo!'

'You should have more respect,' snapped Quil.

'He never took me seriously in life,' said Sekobi with a shrug. 'I see no need to take him seriously in death. He's the one up there, after all. You'll never see me in a cage like that.'

Quil went to respond, but at that point Sylvindor cried out suddenly:

'We really need to get out of—'

And then he stopped, and the air seemed to be sucked out of his sentence. Looking down, the tip of a barbed arrow was sticking out from his chest. He looked shocked. Quil drew her sword.

Then, a deafening peal of screams launched from every corner of the plaza.

'It's a trap!' shouted Sekobi. 'Form a circle – they're coming from all sides!'

Azra leapt into position, seeing shapes already coming towards them – small, toad-like figures which she knew must be goblins.

But Quil didn't go to the post. Instead she strode forward, hacking down two goblins before scooping up the gasping Sylvindor. Fending off three more attackers, she returned to the others.

'I can fight!' Sylvindor coughed, and struggled to draw his sword.

'Get behind me!' shouted Quil, pulling him back.

'Let him fight,' called Sekobi, brandishing his falx at the oncoming goblins. 'We'll need it!'

He met the first wave head on, his blade slicing through the air, and several goblin bodies with it. Those he missed, Azra thrust her sword at, cutting at least one down. Behind them, Quil parried and struck the oncoming creatures, while Sylvindor, now bleeding profusely, still wrestled with his scabbard.

Another wave came. This time, Azra thought quickly. Just as the goblins were upon her, she vanished, reappearing behind them and cutting the backs of their legs with one sweep of her sword.

'Very good!' shouted Sekobi, who fought off one attacker, then waved his arm, conjuring sparks around it, before throwing them like a ball into the ground. The ball exploded, sending light this way and that, and knocking the goblins off their feet.

Sylvindor had now got his sword in his hand. 'You must go on!' he said, weakly. 'I will hold them off!'

'Don't be stupid, boy!' snarled Quil, running through yet another goblin. But Sylvindor wasn't listening. Using the post to push off, he propelled himself forward, shouting 'For the trees!'

Azra saw that, even while wounded, Sylvindor fought with exceptional skill, weaving his way through the goblin axes and clubs, cutting and thrusting as he did. But he was weak, and could not move as well as he wanted. A goblin blade landed in his leg, and a loud snapping sound resonated with the elf's shriek of pain.

'Run!' he shouted, as an axe caught in his side.

Quil turned to Sekobi and Azra, frozen between escaping and staying.

'He's already dead,' declared Sekobi. 'Follow me while the...'

But Azra reacted instinctively. The energy swarmed into her arms and hands, and with a single wind up she sent a bolt of fire through the goblin horde surrounding Sylvindor. It lit them up, then caught a brazier at the far side, knocking it to the floor and spreading fire all around. The goblins shrieked and screamed, and scurried away. Then Azra blinked, and in a moment she was by Sylvindor's side, holding him as he collapsed to the floor.

The elf's breathing was short. Blood ran freely from his mouth, his chest, his leg. He looked up at Azra with his large, blue eyes.

'You should ... have ... gone...' he murmured.

Azra stroked his hair, and hushed him. She looked up at Sekobi.

'Can't you *do* something?'

Quil was urgently pulling a flask out from her pack, but Sekobi shook his head. 'A healing potion will only sustain his pain,' he said, solemnly. 'Please leave him, Marsali.'

Azra held Sylvindor close, feeling his body grow colder. His eyes remained fixed on her, and he managed what may have been a smile. 'Ad ... ventu... ture...' he whispered. And then, he was very still.

11

Hidden magic

Quil was angry. She threw her pack straight at Sekobi, then strode away. In a rage, she took up her sword, still covered in the goblin's blood, and swung it at the post suspending Moshab's cage. She struck it, with a loud clang, then again, then again. Then finally, with all her strength, the last blow knocked it so hard that there was a large snapping sound, and the post gave way, sending the cage above, and the skeletal remains inside, crashing to the ground.

Then Quil stood, breathing heavily. 'He was just a child...' she said, hoarsely.

Sekobi went to say something, but thought better of it.

Azra was still holding her friend's body, but the noise seemed to have shifted it somehow. In fact, she noticed the coldness was slowly receding. Looking down, the elf's eyes had closed. But the wound on his chest – the gaping wound from the goblin's axe – seemed somehow smaller now.

Sekobi came over. 'We need to go,' he said. 'We ... wait, what the...?'

He had seen it too. Sylvindor's leg was no longer bleeding, but was instead now only a small cut. In fact, as they both watched, it could almost be that the wounds were ... healing themselves.

'Quil!' Sekobi shouted. 'The healing potion! Now!'

Quil saw what was happening, but stood still, startled.

'The potion! Ah, never mind...' Sekobi found the flask that Quil had earlier discarded, and hurriedly held it to Sylvindor's lips. The liquid poured into his mouth and over his lips, mixing with the blood and turning a curious colour of dark yellow. 'Come on...' Sekobi urged.

Azra held Sylvindor tight. 'Come on, Syl,' she said. 'Back you come.'

As the healing potion worked its way into him, the blood began to dissolve, and he coughed, then spewed phlegm over Azra's hand.

'His wounds are closing faster than I've ever seen,' said Sekobi, and he sounded not only pleased but also fascinated. 'So, our little elf had magic all along. He kept that hidden well...'

'Come on, Syl,' Azra repeated. And she could feel the warmth returning to his body.

Quil alone stayed back. 'He was dead,' she said, in a choked voice.

'He must have started healing just in time,' remarked Sekobi, taking over from Azra in gently holding the elf as he began to regain consciousness.

'Maybe it's the Warren,' Azra suggested, standing up and looking for some water to give him. 'Maybe whatever power he had is stronger here.'

'Hidden powers,' Quil said. 'Clearly there's more to our elf than meets the eye.'

She frowned, thoughts clearly turning in her mind. Azra took to gathering their things. Sekobi was still checking on Sylvindor. Azra's well-trained ears overheard him talking, quietly. 'That's it, boy, you can make it back. Take your time, you've lost a lot of blood...' And then, as Quil and Azra moved off, he continued, only for Sylvindor to hear: 'You know, I can help you with this gift. I can make you *stronger*...'

Azra caught up with Quil, who was scoping out the next passageway. The adventurer seemed relieved that Sylvindor had survived, but surprisingly also somewhat frustrated.

'I've just spent days risking my life keeping that elf alive and all the time he could just...'

'It still hurt him,' pointed out Azra.

'Yes,' said Quil. 'He was always going to learn that one day. I wonder whether this little trick is why Vane was so insistent on him coming along. I'm beginning to think that we all have a role to play down here.'

'What do you mean?'

'She had planned this all so extensively. Maps, timings, seeking us all out. I don't think any of us are down here by chance.'

Azra shrugged. 'Do you think Grug was better at killing goblins?'

At this, Quil smiled for the first time in a while. 'You would hope.'

'Though he wouldn't be much good getting through some of these tunnels.'

'No,' agreed Quil. 'No ... and as you mention it, this is the way that Vane wanted us to take.' She thought for a moment. 'I mean, the route we took in the last level, a giant would never have made it through there...'

They looked at each other.

'...was Grug ever meant to come with us...?' Azra asked.

'I think there may be mysteries yet to unfold for this plan, my young thief,' Quil replied. 'It may be wise we keep our blades close.'

Azra nodded. She looked back over the plaza, and the piles of shrunken bodies strewn all over. *That's a lot of goblins*, she thought. And she wondered if Quil had ever seen so many in her previous times in the Warren.

'I've seen hordes, but never this many,' Quil said, as if reading her mind. 'Something must have rattled them.'

'Will they be back?'

'Not where we're going.'

'To the dragon's lair?'

Quil grimaced, and nodded. 'There'll be far worse than goblins on the way.' Then she called over to Sekobi. 'Can he walk?'

'I can, I can ...' Sylvindor struggled to get to his feet.

'He'll need help,' warned Sekobi. 'I can try and support him, but we'll need to move slowly. And quietly.'

He hoisted the elf up, supporting his shoulder, and they moved forward carefully.

Quil watched. 'You were all for running not five minutes ago, Sekobi. Why so keen to slow down now?'

'Things change,' he muttered. 'As well you know. Just ask Moshab over there. And besides,' he shot her a look, which held more meaning than Azra could tell. 'I'm not completely unknown for my acts of charity down here.'

'Ah, so you're a hero now?' Quil was unimpressed. 'I came here to do a job. Not end up in some goblin trap.'

Sylvindor wheezed an interjection. 'I'll be ... fine. I'm feeling ... better... already...'

He didn't look fine. While the wounds were healing, Azra could see he was pale and weak from losing so much blood. At the house, Vane had emphasised the need for timeliness in executing their plan. The goblin attack would surely slow them down.

'Perhaps he should stay here,' said Azra. 'Someone can stay with him until he recovers.'

'In the middle of a goblin battleground?' Sekobi responded. 'Hardly a cosy inn with a fire, is it?'

'She's right, though,' said Quil. 'There are four of us now. Perhaps two of us can finish the job, and the others can get back to the surface.'

'We're too far in now,' said Sekobi. 'He's as much chance of making it back through the higher levels as he has the lower ones. The problem is the same whichever way we go.'

Quil looked frustrated. 'I'm just saying, we need to all come out of this alive. And perhaps there's a better chance of it if we split up...'

Sekobi fixed her with a sudden stare. 'And perhaps there's a better chance of half the group making themselves very rich in the process...'

Quil scoffed. 'Oh, come on, what are you accusing me of? Do you think I want gold? Is that why you think I'm here? *I'll* stay and look after the elf, if that's what you're worried about.'

'We *stay together*,' Sekobi said, firmly. Then he turned to Azra. 'What does the thief say? Hers is the casting vote.'

Azra did not like the fact they were staying in the same spot for so long, and while Quil and Sekobi had debated, she had been looking over to the remains, with their curious green boots, and wondering if this was their fate too, to end up as landmarks in the dangerous levels of the Warren. If so, perhaps she should have invested in some more colourful footwear. Then she thought of something.

'The cage – can we use it?'

'What?' Quil and Sekobi asked together.

'Until Syl gets his strength back ... we could use it as a kind of stretcher, I think.'

Sylvindor widened his eyes at her. 'You want to put me in a *cage*?'

Frustrated, Azra vanished over to the cage. Shaking out the remains of Moshab, she picked it up, and vanished back with it in her hands.

'If we carry it on its side, he can sit on the bars, see. Two carry it, one leads.'

Sekobi gave a little laugh. 'Makes sense.'

Quil nodded. 'Yes ... just until he's feeling better. We need all our eyes and ears open for the next part of the journey.'

Sylvindor was less keen, but once Quil had ripped the cage door off completely, and assured him again he would not be locked in, and it was just a way of transporting him, he stepped inside the sideways cage and sat down.

'I'll take first lead,' said Sekobi. 'I know these passages better than anyone, I think.'

Quil rolled her eyes, and heaved one end of the cage up. Azra took up the other side. As an elf, Sylvindor was light enough, but the cage itself was awkward to carry – not as awkward as attempting to lift him without it, but still awkward.

'Come on,' said Sekobi. 'We have a dragon to kill.'

As they set off down a dark walkway, Azra only then realised that she had just vanished holding such a large object. She had never done that before. Clearly the Warren was affecting her. Nobody else seemed to have noticed, though, so she kept walking.

12

Before the dragon's lair

'We're behind time. How long will Vane wait?'

Quil was adjusting her grip on the cage, clearly annoyed that Sekobi remained in front of the party.

'How can you tell we're behind time?' Azra asked.

'I've spent enough time down here to feel the passing of the hours,' Quil replied. 'Even this far down.'

'The flowing streams – see them? The ones that glow,' whispered Syl, twisting around to Azra. 'They glow more red in the night time, and pale in the day.'

'How do you know that?' queried Azra.

Syl smiled and nodded his head back towards Quil, to indicate where he had learned this.

To Sekobi's credit, he had been kept busy in the lead position. Now they were deep into the ground, and the walls of the passages around them had long since ceased to be the angular, designed pillars and walls of the higher levels. This was a labyrinth of twisting tunnels cut out of the rock by races long since deceased, and Sekobi guided them with a small orb of light summoned above his head. But there seemed to be goblins around every corner – sometimes one, sometimes three or four. All were felled by Sekobi's falx, or a sharp shock spell.

Quil was fine to carry the cage, although clearly uncomfortable at being unable to reach her sword as quickly as she wanted. Even in the darkness and shadows, it was clear that Sylvindor's battle scars had healed almost completely, but he was still weak from blood loss, and had also broken his leg.

'The bones take longer,' he had said, before apologising again, and they continued, trudging with Sylvindor balanced on the upturned cage, while Sekobi defended them as best he could.

They reached an open, small chamber with an arched roof and three passageways leading into more darkness, a silver stream trickling through the middle.

'We should rest here,' said Sekobi, and the others placed the cage on the floor with some relief. 'If we follow the stream, the dragon's lair is only a short way away.'

Azra breathed out. The air was a little fresher here, and after carrying the cage so long she was tired. The idea that they were nearly at their destination was good news – if she ignored the bit about the dragon, and focused on the gold instead.

Sylvindor lifted himself up off his carrier, and gingerly stepped on his foot, putting his hands on the wall for balance. 'Better,' he said to himself.

'Can you walk?' asked Azra.

Sylvindor flexed his leg a little. 'I ... think so.'

'Quite a recovery,' noted Sekobi. 'The benefit of being an elf is you won't put too much weight on the leg, I suppose.'

Sylvindor managed a smile, but looked concerned. 'But I won't be fast,' he said. 'I won't be as...' and he waved his hand, indicating a sword fight. 'I'm useless now.'

'You have other skills, my boy. Other skills that can be just as useful.' Sekobi wiped the sweat from his brow and slung his falx on to his back. 'If only we'd known earlier.'

Quil, checking out the tunnels, grunted. 'If Vane's maps were correct, we can loop back from the dragon to this magical doorway,' she said, then added: '*If* the maps were correct...'

'They've been true so far,' Sekobi said, taking a swig from his water bottle. 'I'm more concerned about how we get chests of gold from the lair to the doorway with the number of goblins around. We'll be easy targets. And they seem remarkably more persistent than we planned for.'

Sylvindor was sat still, and Azra realised he was listening, using his elven senses to project down the tunnels around them. 'There's movement,' he said.

Quil went to draw her sword.

'No, it's far off. I think – I think they are behind us.'

Quil relaxed her grip on the sword hilt, but remained alert.

'I don't like it,' she said. 'So many goblins. Where are all the other creatures?'

'You said they wouldn't follow us here,' said Azra, which wasn't meant to sound like an accusation, but Quil simply raised her shoulders. 'That's the thing. They shouldn't. This isn't their territory.'

'It's been a while since we were last here,' said Sekobi. 'Maybe things change.'

Quil frowned. 'The Warren never changes.'

'I'm more concerned about the dragon,' Sylvindor said, taking the water bottle that Sekobi offered him.

'He makes a good point,' Sekobi said. 'But I have a plan. Rather than attempt to fight the dragon, I suggest we take a stealthy approach. Two of us can get into the lair, sneak past the dragon and retrieve the gold.'

'Who would go?' asked Quil, suspiciously.

'Well, the elf is healing, and walks noiselessly,' replied Sekobi. 'And I know the passages, and the way out.'

Quil snorted. 'Only a day back you were criticising me for trying to divide the group. Now you're saying you will go and take the treasure alone?'

'Yes. You and the thief can hold the rear should the goblins find us.'

'But wouldn't I be better going for the treasure?' Azra said. 'I can just...'

'Sylvindor will be of no use in a fight now, even if he can walk,' said Sekobi. 'You guard, we steal, and then we meet at the door.'

'The door which only you can open?' Quil inquired.

Sekobi looked at Azra quickly, then back to Quil.

'How else are we to do this and come out alive?' he cried.

'I've never seen a dragon,' said Sylvindor, perhaps in an effort to quieten the discussion a little. 'Are they really that hard to kill?'

'Impossible,' said Sekobi, flatly. 'And I don't say that from lack of trying.'

This could have been useful to know earlier, thought Azra to herself. She thought back to their planning discussions in the house, which seemed so long ago now.

'Vane didn't say we had to kill it,' she said. 'If we were to just take gold from these levels, as much as we can carry, and bring it out of the Warren, then surely the job would be done? What would the difference be to the Baron? If there are goblins all around us, and Syl is lame...'

Unexpectedly, both Sekobi and Quil turned on her.

'I didn't come all this way, and risk this much, for a few gold coins,' Sekobi hissed. 'That treasure the dragon guards is like no other. A few chests may be all we need. But they must be the dragon's chests.'

Azra looked at Quil. 'But you said you weren't here for the treasure,' she said, stoutly.

'I'm here for something greater, Azra.' Quil replied. 'I'm here to defeat the Warren, do you understand? To complete it. To finish the game. *That's* what will bring the Warren down. And that goes through the dragon's lair. Which we will do – *all* of us.'

After a short while, they were ready to move on. Sylvindor insisted he could walk – or hobble – and using the rock surfaces to balance he could now keep up with the rest. As they departed, Azra picked up the cage a final time and pushed it into the mouth of the tunnel they had entered through, wedging the ends in place.

'That won't hold back anyone,' warned Quil, as the others pressed on.

'It will let us know if anything comes through, though,' Azra replied.

Quil nodded. 'Good thinking.' Then she added: 'You see, you don't always need magic to get things done.'

'Hmm,' Azra had, in fact, gripped the bars so that the metal had become very hot. She didn't know how long the effect would last, but it would give any goblin running into it a bit of a burn. Quil hadn't noticed, though, and as they both followed the rest of the party, she said in a low voice: 'You could do well with your skills. Outside, I mean. You fight well. You think well. You could sell those services. Outside, I mean.'

Azra didn't reply. Nobody had ever suggested this to her before. But then, nobody had wanted her around.

'He'll tell you otherwise,' Quil went on. 'Use the magic, grow your power, I'll make you great, the same old story. He probably even told you that back in the house. But that way only leads to bad things. A twisted darkness.'

Azra looked around the gloomy tunnel they were stepping through.

'Seems we're already there,' she suggested.

'*This isn't a joke*, Azra. You're too good to be a thief. You've got talent. Make it count.'

'Quiet back there!' shushed Sekobi, as they caught up.

They followed the stream downwards. After a while, the tunnels began to broaden, and they were once again in something that looked more constructed, yet still oddly shaped and strange, as if these corridors had been built by a civilisation unknown to the world above.

And then, they were there. A large gate stood before them, lit by a flame which could only be sustained through some unseen magic. Ancient bars with jagged edges blocking the way through.

Quil consulted her map. 'That way,' she pointed into the darkness to the right. 'That's the doorway, a few turns along. And beyond this gate – well, I think we all know.'

They paused for a moment, all of them realised they were now in the final stage of Vane's grand plan. Sylvindor, resting against the wall of the passage, was listening again.

'I can hear something,' he said.

'A dragon,' said Sekobi, taking a deep breath.

'No – smaller. I can't quite make out where it is.' Sylvindor screwed up his face in concentration. 'So many memories here … it's so old. Perhaps some of us should stay back and...'

'Snap out of it!' Quil chided him. 'You said the goblins were behind us. We go through the gate together.'

And she took hold of a wrought iron lever set into the stone of the archway, and heaved it. A grating screech filled the air, as the iron spikes began to move upwards.

'So much for stealth,' said Sekobi, shrugging, as Sylvindor held his ears.

'Come on, Syl,' said Azra. 'We'll need your sword.'

They entered under the arch, and immediately they were in better-lit paths, but they wound curiously just as the carved walls did.

'It's a labyrinth of sorts,' said Sekobi. 'Don't be distracted by it. Keep your sense of direction and we'll get to the lair. You'll know when we're there...'

13

The gold and the glory

For a moment, the scene that greeted the four inside the dragon's lair left them speechless.

For Azra, her eyes first went to the gold. Piles and piles of it, reaching up the far wall of a huge stone cathedral, dripping out of chests and covering the floor.

But from there her gaze went to the middle of the room. There, a colossal shape, curled in a half-moon, took up nearly all the space. It was a dragon. Or at least, it had been.

'It's ... dead?' Sylvindor, his sword at the ready, looked in a mixture of awe and uncertainty.

'Impossible...' breathed Sekobi. 'It must have simply ... died of old age.'

The dragon was mostly skeleton now. The jaw of its skull was open, with its wicked teeth, the size of Azra herself, trained up towards the vaulted ceiling above.

'Yes, Sekobi,' said Quil. 'Old age. Because another adventurer could not have possibly done what you failed to do.'

She put her sword to the floor and leaned on the hilt, looking content with herself.

Sekobi pointed to the floor, which was covered with more bones and skeletal corpses. 'So few got this far, and all those who tried ended up there. Only one survived, and that was me!' he said.

Quil simply smiled, triumphantly. 'Perhaps only two survived. Even if the world seemed to insist I was dead.'

Azra thought Sekobi was angry at first, then looked confused, before finally twisting his face into a smile – but an honest smile, and for the first time, it might have even been affection for his fellow warrior.

Sylvindor, meanwhile, had his mouth wide open. 'You *killed* that?'

'Perhaps,' replied Quil. 'Perhaps, as Sekobi says, it simply died of old age. Dragons do get old at some point, after all.'

'Well. Congratulations, Marsali Quil. There's a story for the taverns, and no mistake. But why did we not know about this before?'

'To what end?' Quil replied. 'The gold – there's far too much of it. How would one person get that back to the surface? Carry a chest past a goblin horde or two?'

Amid the exchange, Azra thought she could hear something stirring. Somewhere in the gold – she had her eyes back on the gold. But the room was carrying the echoes of Sekobi questioning Quil, and Sylvindor uttering his admiration, and it was difficult to tell. That was, until Sylvindor turned to Azra, and she saw his face turn to terror, and he shouted: 'Watch out!'

Azra blinked, and in a second she was up on the wall, clinging to a sconce holding a lit torch. She saw below her, just where she had been standing, a jagged sword was protruding – a sword which would have been in her back had she not vanished just in time.

The sword was held, though, by a creature she had never seen before. It had seemed to emerge out of the bones themselves, and now stood, taller than a man, a skeletal knight. And it was not alone.

Around them, more figures began to emerge from the floor, rising up through some unknown force, collecting fragments and shards of bone as they did, until six such skeletal knights stood, ready to fight. Two held long, metallic spears, and the others were armed with the same jagged swords that had been aimed at Azra.

Sekobi looked at Quil, who simply shrugged. Then, taking up her sword, she charged at the nearest knight.

Sylvindor whirled into action, parrying the blow of one skeleton and slicing his blade at another. Sekobi fired a blast of air from his hand, sending a knight staggering backwards, while he engaged the last in hand-to-hand combat.

Azra focused on her attacker, and just as it started to move on Quil, she leapt forward, bringing her sword down and splitting the creature's skull in two.

Quil, meanwhile, succeeded in disarming her opponent, and ran her sword through its chest, before bringing it out through its side, shattering the skeleton's body as she did so.

Spinning around while brandishing his falx, Sekobi cut the skeletal knight he fought cleanly into two, before running to help Sylvindor. While the elf was ably holding off his two attackers, his lack of mobility meant that he could not find an opening to bring them down.

But there was still one more, and it charged towards Azra. Azra focused on its chest, and feeling a surge of energy in her arms, in a single moment felt herself project forward, as if she was vanishing again. But this time, she stayed where she was, and instead a ball of space exploded from inside the knight, sending parts of his body in all directions.

As Sylvindor felled the final skeleton, Quil cast a glance at Azra.

'Couldn't you just use a sword like the rest of us?' she asked, dryly. Then she turned to Sekobi with a glint in her eye. 'Was that what you were trying to do, Sekobi?'

'It doesn't matter,' said Sekobi, regaining his breath. '*That's* what matters.'

And he pointed to the gold.

'We'll never move all of that,' said Quil.

'No. But we can move as much as we can,' the trickster replied.

'How?'

Sekobi scooped up the two spears that the skeletal knights had held. 'We use these. Pile as much as you can into those chests. We should be able to carry two chests with these, if we hook them through the sides. Then two can carry and two can fight, if needed.'

Azra was impressed at the quick thinking, which confirmed her suspicion that, like her, this was not Sekobi's first robbery.

There was no argument this time. They worked quickly and quietly, gathering up the valuables which Azra had never seen the likes of before. Following the plan, Azra and Sekobi took the weight of the treasure on the two spears, while Quil led the way back to the gated archway. From there, they turned and followed the passageway, until after some more time Quil stopped.

'This is it. The moment of truth.'

'Is this definitely the place?' Sylvindor asked Sekobi. He nodded.

The wall could have been like any other – a short dead end, cut out of the main passageway but leading nowhere at all. Indeed, its only distinguishing features were some uneven markings. And as Sekobi raised a glowing orb over his hand, he traced out what looked like a curved door.

'Go on, then, Sekobi,' said Quil, sardonically. 'You didn't get your dragon, but you can still open a door for us.'

Sekobi looked at the wall, and his face was one of thought and concentration.

'You do know how to open this?' Quil asked. 'Tell me you know...'

Sekobi shook his head. 'I do, but there's no sense in going just yet. We can get another two chests here if we go back now.'

Quil punched the wall, angrily. 'We are behind time as it is! Two chests is enough!'

'For all we've been through, we should leave with more!' Sekobi retorted.

But at that moment, a crashing noise from somewhere far off echoed through the tunnels, and the distant screech of a goblin being burned.

'They're here!' cried Sylvindor.

'Then we must move quickly,' Sekobi said, and before anyone could stop him, he grabbed hold of the two spears and bolted back down the passageway, back to the dragon's lair.

Quil flung her hands into the air. 'We can't open the door without him ... Get after him, Azra! There's time before the goblins find us, but it won't be that long. We'll stay here and cover your return.'

Azra nodded, and vanished. She reappeared behind Sekobi just as he reached the archway.

'I thought you'd agree with me,' he said, not stopping.

They reached the lair far quicker now they knew the way. As they hurriedly gathered more gold into two more chests, Azra said: 'I don't agree. And I don't know why I'm helping you.'

'Why else are we here?' replied Sekobi. 'I want the gold. As do you. As do we all.'

'Quil says she doesn't.'

'Quil wants glory. And glory and gold are much the same thing, see? They all mean the same, in the end.'

'And what is that?'

'Escape,' Sekobi said adamantly, as he loaded handfuls of gold into the chest. 'Escape for a moment. Escape from the inevitable passing of time and the loneliness of our existence. Quil may talk of her noble deeds, and her famous sword skills, but it's no different from you stealing a purse to buy bread. Escape for a moment. This is why they all come here, after all.'

And then, quite unexpectedly, he stopped what he was doing and looked at her. And Azra saw that there seemed to be genuine concern in his eyes.

'It's why you should never have come here.'

Azra looked back at him. 'What do you mean? I can do things here that I was never able to do outside. I can...'

Sekobi shook his head. 'So. That's why you don't know why you're helping me. Not because of the plan. You mean you don't know why we're going through with it. You mean you want to stay.'

Azra was defensive. 'No – no, I ... it's just...'

'You feel it,' Sekobi rolled his eyes, but not in disgust, more in sympathy. 'The Warren'.

'Not that. I can travel further here. I feel more ... more powerful.' Then something fell into place in Azra's mind, something she'd been trying to make sense of since the second level. 'And I don't want to lose it, by going outside.'

Sekobi said nothing at first, but nodded, with that odd smile he had. 'Ah, I understand,' he said, after a while. 'But there's something you should know.'

'Oh?'

'What I said, about the magic having more effect on the lower levels...'

'Yes – I felt it. I felt it as soon as I left the first level.'

Sekobi let out a long breath. 'It's true. But Azra, the magic gets stronger ... far, far down. Seventh, eighth level. Not the second.'

Azra was stunned.

'But – but I could vanish further. I could make a flame. I could...'

'You could,' Sekobi agreed. 'But not because of the Warren.'

Then he leaned into her, putting his face up to hers, and whispered: '*It's what you are.*'

They didn't speak, but silently hoisted two more treasure chests on to the litter, and hurried back as fast as they could, all the while keeping the chests balanced. As they reached the door, Quil was already standing ready with Sylvindor close by, swords drawn.

'Get that door open!' she urged. 'They'll be here any moment!'

14

Daylight

Sekobi set to work on the door, pressing his hands against the surface, his head down, muttering an incantation. Azra stood back, her head on a swivel to the tunnels either side. The goblins would no doubt be here soon. The clamour of their movement was getting louder. Quil and Sylvindor both stood ready, a little further along each direction of the passage, the elf still a little uncertain on his feet, but insistent he could now fight.

Quil called back to Sekobi. 'So? Is it a magic door or not? We don't have long.'

It was magic alright, Azra could feel it. The warm glow radiating from its contours was hard to ignore, but beyond that sensation she could not make sense of it. This would be old, old magic. She hoped Sekobi knew a way to interpret it.

Then, the goblins were upon them. The passages were narrow, but they came from both sides, and they came in hordes. Quil set to work defending their position, and Azra took up a place next to Syl, keeping slightly back from his quick blade, but thrusting her sword in when an enemy came close enough.

'What's happening?' shouted Quil. 'Why isn't it opening?'

'This is ancient magic,' Sekobi snapped back. 'The spells are entangled and submerged.'

'*Can you get it open?*'

'With time...'

We don't have time, thought Azra. Even though the goblins were not difficult to fight, the sheer number of them would soon overwhelm them. She could see that even Quil was beginning to tire.

Felling one more creature, Azra jumped back to where Sekobi was, surrounded by the gold-laden chests.

Vanisher

'Can I help?' she asked.

'No,' replied Sekobi. 'No, the elf perhaps, if he was more attuned, but not you. The magic is too complex...'

Azra looked at the door, then at the black mass of goblins bearing down on either side. And in that moment, she made a decision.

'I can,' she said. And she placed her hands on two of the chest handles, focused in front of her, and felt the warmth of the magic around her surge into her hands.

She had no idea, of course, what was behind the door. Vane had promised them a cave. She had never vanished into a place she had not seen, but there was no other choice. And when she appeared, a split second later, she was in total darkness. Her arms instantly ached, as if she had dragged both treasure chests for miles. But she realised that she had done it – she had got through the door, and with the treasure in hand.

She could hear the faint noise of the battle through the stone surface behind her. Determinedly, she vanished back.

Sekobi looked astonished. 'Where have you be—?

Azra simply continued, taking the last two chests with her, then back. Quil and Sylvindor had retreated into the alcove, and Sekobi was helping them. Using the last of the energy in her, Azra laid her hands on all three, and in an instant they found themselves in the dark cave beyond.

As Sekobi sparked a light from his hand, Azra fell to the floor, exhausted.

'Good work,' said Sekobi, patting her on the head. 'I would have got the door open eventually, but...'

'We can only hope that Vane has kept her side of the plan,' said Quil, looking at their surroundings. They were in a cave, but a very different one to the tunnels they had previously been in. This was natural, but there were signs where pickaxes had hollowed the walls out further.

'We have to wait for Azra,' said Sylvindor. 'She's worn out.'

'There will be time to rest after we've got out of here,' said Quil. As she stepped forward, a crunch underfoot made her stop and look down.

'What's this, more skeletons?' asked Sekobi. He brought the light closer to the floor, and the two of them peered down.

'These look like dwarves,' said Quil, curiously.

'Why were dwarves fighting down here?' asked Sylvindor.

'It doesn't look like they were fighting...' said Sekobi. 'I think it wise we keep going.'

'But Azra...' started Sylvindor, from somewhere in the darkness.

Azra stood up, her head swimming a little as she felt the warmth slowly returning to her hands.

'It's fine, it's fine. Can we lift all of these chests at once?'

'No,' said Sekobi. Despite his light spell, it was still gloomy, and difficult to make out their surroundings. 'We got four out, yes? So we can take two between us. We'll move those for now and come back for the others.'

'I can't see them all,' Quil said. Azra went to take one of the chest handles, but as soon as she pulled on it, she realised she was still too tired to lift it. Sekobi watched her.

'Okay, we'll take one. And we'll hope that Vane has brought a cart...'

Leaving the other chests where they were, the party ventured forward. The passage wound to the right, then slowly ascended, before it took a steep upward climb. After their many battles, even Quil struggled to keep the chest, weighed down with so much treasure, upright.

Finally, they reached another passage, which was lit by a strange, narrow ray of light that seemed to come from the end.

Sekobi went forward first. 'Aha,' he called back. 'It seems I was right.'

Azra wearily joined him. She could now see that the mouth of the passageway seemed to have been bricked up. Only a few of the bricks had been knocked out, but from the other side, letting the daylight through a small window.

Azra touched the bricks. 'The dwarves – they were closed off down here. Someone shut them in.'

Sekobi nodded, grimly. 'What did Vane say? The dwarven miners did not survive the discovery of the cave ... Well, it seems that we now know why. Come, help me. I'm sure you could squeeze through that hole, but we'll need room for the rest of us.'

They worked the bricks loose, opening the passageway up to the world again. Finally, they had enough space to step through, with Quil and Sylvindor bringing the chest with them.

Azra turned and saw the sky for the first time in days. The sting of the sunlight burned into her eyes, and she shielded them with her arm. Slowly adjusting after her time below the surface, the world outside was green, bright and cold. She could now see that they were at the foot of the Screaming Mountains, with wild grass stretching out before them and an ocean behind.

Next to the beaten path, clearly not often used, a cart was parked, with some hooded figures standing nearby.

'Vane's brought some muscle,' said Sekobi. 'Thank goodness we don't have to lift this much further.'

'Where is Vane?' asked Sylvindor.

Quil put down the chest. 'I want to get out of here quickly,' she said, and strode forward with Sekobi.

'There,' she said, pointing the chest at the cave mouth. 'The rest is inside. Have your men load up the cart.'

Sylvindor went to follow. 'Come on, we can go now,' he said. But Azra was hesitant.

'I'm not sure everything's right here...' she began.

No sooner had she spoken than the hooded figures threw off their cloaks to reveal tabards of black with silver chevrons – the uniform of the Baron of Kaveshvill. They drew battle axes, and the nearest pointed at the adventurers and ordered: 'Drop your weapons!'

'It's a trap!' shouted Quil.

'They're not taking the gold now,' snarled Sekobi, reaching for his falx.

The Baron's guards did not wait long for the adventurers to surrender. Clearly under order to attack at the slightest sign, they ran straight at Sekobi and Quil. Fuelled by the fire of battle, Quil immediately set about them, and Sekobi's falx whistled through the air, cutting down their assailants.

'The gold!' he shouted back to Sylvindor. 'Get the gold on the cart!'

The elf disappeared back into the cave. But no sooner had he done so then the thunder of galloping hooves announced a company of horsemen charging from their right. Azra spun around, and saw at least twenty horses coming towards them, fanning out as if to encircle them.

'Run, Azra!' Quil commanded. 'Get out of here!'

'*But the gold!*' screamed Sekobi. Quil grabbed hold of him and shouted: 'We have to leave!'

Azra realised that she was right. To fight a group of axemen was one thing, but to take on that many mounted soldiers, especially given how tired they all were, would be senseless. Sylvindor was still trying to get hold of the treasure chest, but Azra ran up to him.

'We have to go, Syl, now.'

'But what about Quil and Sekobi?'

Azra looked over her shoulder. In fact, Quil and Sekobi had both already started to run, in different directions, to evade the oncoming charge.

'They'll survive!' And with that, Azra placed her hands on Syl's arms. With the last energy she had left, they vanished.

15

Escape to the trees

When Azra awoke, she was in a forest. The delicate sound of crisp birdsong filled the air, and the greenery was so bright in contrast to the dull shadows of the Warren, she thought for a moment she may be still asleep, and dreaming.

Then she saw Sylvindor, who was doing exercises on a tree branch.

'You're awake!' he said. 'Good!'

Azra sat up, rubbing her head. 'Where are we?'

'This is called the Rosegrove. It's in the northern part of Haemir.'

Azra looked around in bewilderment. 'The great elven forest?'

Sylvindor nodded, then jumped down to the floor, and perched on a large tree root next to Azra.

'It was ... the only place I could think of,' he said, in a way that sounded almost apologetic.

'What do you mean? Did we vanish here?'

'No, no. We landed only a small way from the riders. But we were behind some rocks and boulders, and you had passed out. So I hid us, and waited for them to pass by. They searched the caves, and when they couldn't find any of us, they shouted that they must search every town and village in the land, and that we must be brought to justice.'

Azra sighed. 'What happened to the gold?'

'Gone.' The elf shook his head, dejectedly. 'They carted what they could find off. But a while later some men came back with another cart – they had been sent to check if there was any more left in the case.'

'Where did they look?'

'What do you mean? Oh, they went into the cave. While they were in there, I carried you to the cart and was able to drive away.'

Azra laughed a little. 'I didn't have you as a thief,' she said.

'It was the only way I could move you,' he said.

'Why didn't you just leave?'

Sylvindor frowned. 'I couldn't have done that,' he said, solemnly.

Azra scowled. 'You could have got yourself killed. Again.'

'It was the right thing to do! And anyway, you got us out of the Warren. I did fear you'd left us after you'd gone for so long, but still, it wouldn't have been right to just leave you after using your strength to help. Anyway, where was I?' Sylvindor wanted to carry on with his story. 'Oh yes, they were all over the place, the Baron's guards. I looked in Anson, and it was all but taken over with black and silver flags. It was no idle threat, Azra, they really are everywhere, looking for us. I realised that we couldn't go to any settlements. So I headed for the only place I knew they wouldn't go. Back to the elves.'

'Somebody must have betrayed us,' said Azra, feeling an icy cold spread through her body. 'How else did the Baron know we would be there?'

Sylvindor simply shrugged. 'I don't know,' he said. 'At least we got to see the Warren.'

Azra wanted to react angrily to this. After all, they had just lost riches beyond their dreams, and were now being chased by the most powerful man in the land, so it did not seem that there were many silver linings to be had. Still, she was taken aback by Sylvindor's efforts to save her while she had been unconscious, and she also got the sense that while he was glad to be in the safety of the trees, he was quite apprehensive about being back among the elves again. She remembered that he had never talked about why he had left, and had assumed it had not been a friendly departure.

She thanked him for helping her. 'You didn't have to,' she said.

'You warned us just in time,' he said. 'When we left the cave, I mean. You must have a sixth sense for danger. I need to work on reacting quicker to that.' And he tapped the area where the goblin sword had caught him before.

This made Azra laugh. 'What now?' she asked, looking around again. 'Rosegrove? What is it?'

'Just somewhere on the path.'

'The path to where?'

'The path back to my home village.'

Azra stood up, delicately. She had clearly been out for a long time. 'Are they going to be pleased to see you?' she asked. 'You did leave, after all.'

Sylvindor shrugged again, then reached into his pack and fished out some bread for Azra to eat. 'We can only find out,' he said.

After eating, they set off further into the woodland. Soon, Azra could see why the Baron's guards would not come here – it was all but impossible to keep one's bearings, and if she had not had the elf to guide her, she would have been going around in circles for a long time.

Eventually, they arrived at a clearing, where a series of wooden structures came into view. These looked like some kind of stockade, but rather than defending a keep or a tower, they ran around great trees which rose into the sky and disappeared into the thick green canopy above.

Azra immediately became aware that they were not alone. While at first she couldn't see anyone, she felt the stares of a hundred pairs of eyes on her, from all around. She looked up and saw a maze of platforms and gantries connecting the trees together. *The elven village*, she thought.

As they approached, the gate to the stockade opened, and three elves marched out. The first was old, dressed in a long flowing robe. The other two were clearly guards, armed with curved swords and fine bows and arrows. They looked a lot more skilled than goblins, Azra reckoned.

Sylvindor clearly recognised the old elf, but struggled initially to speak. He was clearly tense, trying to make sense of thoughts tangled in his head. It was obvious that he had been gone for a long time, and returning here was not easy. Instead, the elder spoke first.

'Prince Sylvindor. So it is true, you *are* returning to us.'

'Prince?' Azra snapped her head round at her elf companion.

'I—I—return as your humble servant, Master Balris,' said Sylvindor, searching for the right words. 'I am here ... I am here in peace.'

'You better be,' growled one of the guards. Azra reflected that elves were not very good at growling, with their slightly higher-pitched voices, but she didn't question this as the guard did look well-armed.

'Of course! Your brother has been eagerly awaiting since we first received the message!'

'My brother?'

'Why yes, Prince Sylvindor! The brother has missed you so much since your ... your ... dispersion from Haemir. And when the messenger arrived only four days ago with a letter intended only for your eyes, well, there was much excitement that you might be returning.'

'A letter?' Sylvindor looked confused.

'I thought you said you'd not been here for years,' said Azra. 'Why are people sending you notes here?'

Sylvindor shook his head, not knowing. 'Where is this note? Did my brother open it?'

'But of course not. He was curious, of that there is no doubt. But he was more curious, as were we all, as to whether you would return to receive it. And now here you are.'

'And the letter?'

'In your quarters, Prince! Your brother ordered them to be made up just in case. Word has been sent to him – he is out hunting now – but he will return to see you as soon as he hears, of that I have no doubt.'

'So ... we can come in?' Sylvindor asked, meekly.

'You are most welcome!' said the old elf, with a warm smile.

'Then why did you bring Samyar and the guard?'

Samyar, the growling elf, stepped forward.

'You can come in. But not that one.' And he pointed straight at Azra.

'What? Why not my friend?' Sylvindor demanded.

Samyar did not answer, but reached into his cuirass and produced a scroll, which he unfolded with deliberate care in front of Sylvindor.

'Because, absent prince, I suggest you choose your friends more wisely.'

He showed Sylvindor the scroll. It was a poster, one declaring that a villain was at large and wanted for theft and murder. And below the writing promising a reward for their capture was a picture, an inked sketch of a girl's face. And the girl was very unmistakeably Azra.

'This is a mistake,' said Sylvindor, pushing the scroll away. 'We are both here to seek sanctuary in Haemir. This is my companion and we have fought together on quests. I will not hear a word against...'

'This is the ruling,' interrupted Samyar, firmly. 'You may have been gone a long time, Prince, but you know as well as I do that the world of men does not enter Haemir unless the circumstances are exceptional. And if the men outside of the forest venture so far as to warn us of criminals on the loose, then we take those warnings seriously.'

Azra was doing her best to look like she was calm, all the while scanning the area to look for an escape route, and sizing up the guards.

Seeing this, the older elf spoke again. 'The law of men is of no concern to us, girl. You will find no harm while we talk. But we cannot let you into our kingdom, not with the warnings these scrolls give.'

'But it isn't *true!*' exclaimed Sylvindor. 'Why would these scrolls be made?'

Azra bowed her head. She felt defeated. Of all the places for her past to catch up with her, this was the least expected.

'It's alright, Syl. It's alright,' she said. 'Thank you for getting me this far. I think this is where our paths separate.'

'What? No, you will come here as my guest, or we will go back out into the forest together, and find Quil and Sek…'

Azra raised her hand to quieten him. 'This is your home. It's not mine. We will meet again, I'm sure.'

And she gave him a smile.

'It was a good adventure,' she assured him. And he nodded in agreement. 'Look after yourself, Sylvindor,' Azra said. Then, she bid him farewell.

16

The unravelling

She had to find Vane. Vane was the key to this all.

There was only one place to go to. And that's how Azra found herself once again in the port of Blackwater, standing very still in the shadows. Once again, she waited, watching the houses, the windows, listening for any sound of danger. Now, even more than ever before, she needed to make sure that nobody saw her.

This time, she didn't need to go up to the door. Sekobi had been right – her powers had remained strong. It was as if the Warren had unleashed some hidden forces inside her. She could travel further with her vanishing, and the energy in her hands and arms kept warm. She still couldn't quite describe it, but the world felt more ... graspable, now. But even if she had not already seen several of the Baron's guards stalking the streets – the town guards simply got out of their way, and they clearly had authority here to do as they pleased – she didn't need to risk crossing the street. She simply clenched her fists, and in a moment she was standing in the middle of the house, the same house they had contrived the plan in.

It was the same house, that was for sure, but it now looked different. Instead of the sparse but well-kept furnishings, smashed chairs and broken glass littered the floors. Someone had been here, and someone had not been happy when they had.

As Azra stood by the table where Vane had sat, she became aware that she was not alone. There was a slight flicker of movement behind her. Quicker than the other person could react, Azra span around, grabbing them by the neck and pushing them up against the wall next to the lit fire.

It was the little old woman, the one who had first opened the door for her.

Azra scowled. 'Where is she?'

The old woman was choking. 'Not here ... *ach*... not here!'

'Then where has she gone?' Azra repeated, angrily. 'Where is Vane?'

The woman waved her arms a little and wheezed: 'They ... took her!'

She could feel the blood beating in the old woman's neck, faster and faster. Around them, the room was beginning to tremble, and it seemed to move in time with the pulsation in her hands. And as she focused, it was almost as if the whole room was bending around the little old woman, held up against the fireplace.

'Then why are you here? Hathred? Your name was Hathred!'

'I ... *ach* ... I am waiting for *you*...'

Azra relaxed her grip on the old woman. The disfiguring of the room eased.

'What do you mean? Why are you waiting for me?'

The woman breathed out, felt her wrinkled neck with her hand, then smiled a crooked smile. 'Of course you remember my name. Vanishers always have such strong memories. It's how they know where to go when they disappear, I suppose.'

'They took Vane but left you here?' Azra was not interested in the woman's observations.

'Oh, I may not have your powers, but one does not live to three hundred and forty-one years old by not knowing how to hide.'

To Azra's surprise, the woman spoke quite differently to how she had when they had first met. She seemed ... wiser, somehow.

'You didn't hide very well when I came in,' Azra replied.

'Yes, well, I knew it was you, of course. Not many know the ways of the vanishers, but I have lived long enough to know when the fog appears and time slows. Most only see you disappear and reappear, of course – they don't see the warping of reality around you.'

Azra narrowed her eyes. 'You know a lot about vanishing.'

'I know a lot about you, Azra. Vanishers are rare. Once in a generation. I should know. Why else do you think the lady Vane wanted you?'

'I don't know,' said Azra, suspiciously. 'She seemed to have a reason for everything, though.'

'She did!' cackled the woman. 'But they still took her. The Baron's men. They took her back to the palace. They will still be looking for you.'

Azra sighed. So it really was all over.

'I take it the plan was not a success,' the old woman went on, but her voice was now oddly kinder. 'I tried to warn her, but she wouldn't listen. Nevertheless, it seems your trip to the caves perhaps spurred on some of your … skills. Bending rooms, very good. Not many vanishers live long enough to do that. You must be a very powerful breed.'

Azra stepped away. She didn't want to think about it just now. 'Why were you waiting for me?' she asked, again.

'There is a letter for you. Another letter, for your eyes only, which I am to give to you. Just like the one that brought you here in the first place.'

'A letter for me? What does it say?'

'It is sealed, of course. This is not to say I don't know what it says. I don't need to read it! I have always foreseen the path this would take.'

'You might have said something when we were planning…'

'You misunderstand me. I saw this path from long, long before you assembled here in this house. When you hold the knowledge that I do, Azra, you can see how the lines of destiny always intertwine.' The old woman held out a note. Then her face darkened.

'And now I need you to know. This letter, Azra, will lead to your destruction. Just as the first was meant to.'

Azra took the note. Without looking at it, she threw it in the fire.

The old woman's eyes lit up with the flames. 'Good,' she said. 'I knew there would be something more to you, Azra Mujkic.'

Azra watched the parchment burn, and began to think of where she could hide. She would need to leave Bryvania, somehow.

Hathred interrupted her thoughts. 'They will be here soon, the others.'

Azra looked at her. 'How do you know that?'

The old woman scoffed. 'I was not always such a serving maid to delusional nobility, you know! Once, I had a different profession. Once I had knowledge beyond all of your understanding. They knew me as the archivist.'

'The archivist?'

'Yes. How else do you think Vane tracked you all down? How else did she come across the only people capable of carrying out her foolish plan? But what she didn't want to know was the full story. I have known you all since your births, and I have known what binds you all together. And I also know, Azra, that it is the vanisher who alone can break those binds.'

A hundred and one questions flooded into Azra's head, but before she could ask them, the latch on the front door clicked. And from out of the dark hall, a figure strode in purposefully. They stopped when they saw Azra, stood by the fire.

'So you did make it out,' said Quil. 'Good.'

17

An empty room

'The Baron's guards are everywhere,' Quil said, sitting on the stairs and inspecting a gash on her left arm. 'I managed to return to my quarters in Eastmere, and already there were black and silver shields all over the place.'

'Did they see you?' asked Azra, drinking a warm mug of something reassuring that Hathred had made for her.

'They seemed to know where to find me,' Quil said. 'Surrounded the inn. But I managed to get out of a window and escape along the roof. That kept them guessing for long enough for me to grab a horse and find my way here.'

'You're too late,' Azra said. 'Vane has been taken.'

'So I can see,' Quil replied. 'Where is the elf?'

There was a sudden flourish, and from the door a shadow morphed into Sekobi the Trickster.

'He would be back with his tree friends, if he had any sense,' he said. 'And you would be holing up in the furthest reaches of the land, if you had any sense. Not that it would do much good. The Baron has investments in so many of the nobility of Bryvania it would only be a matter of time before he caught up with you. So, as we can see, none of us have any sense. First, we place our trust in a woman and a map. Second, we all end up back here.'

And from behind him, he yanked in Sylvindor, pushing him into the room.

'Some of whom don't even have the sense to keep under cover as they arrive in Blackwater.'

Sylvindor brushed himself down. He looked around, acknowledging the others, then asked: 'But where is Vane?'

'Gone,' said Quil.

'Why are you here, Syl?' Azra asked. 'You were safe in the forest!'

Sylvindor looked uncomfortable. 'I was ... I was worried about you. And besides, the forest is not my home anymore. I couldn't stay there when others may ... need me.'

Idiot, Azra thought to herself. But she found it was not meant in a harsh way. Instead, she was touched at the sentiment.

Sekobi was looking across the room at Hathred. 'Have you pressed the old woman for information?'

'I don't need to,' Quil replied, fiercely. 'We were betrayed. That much is clear. We were sworn to secrecy, and we carried out the plan as well as we might. We had eyes on each other almost the entire time. But who is not among us now? Vane. The one who had it all planned.'

'That makes no sense, though,' said Azra. 'Why would she go to all that bother – the maps, the letters, the planning – only to betray us? Why would the Baron arrest her, if she had betrayed us to him? It makes no sense...'

'It doesn't matter,' said Sekobi, slowly. 'Vane has gone. The gold has gone. Our freedom has gone. We will be hunted down for as long as we remain at large in these lands. If we'd even managed to get one chest out, we could perhaps ... we could find the means to defend ourselves ... but no. We finished with nothing. And it seems to me ... it seems to me now that there is only one place that we could hope for safety.'

And he looked at Quil, with deep regret on his face. Quil looked back, and it seemed to Azra like perhaps she gave a small gesture of recognition, and of acceptance.

'You mean the very place we set out to destroy,' Quil said, sadly.

'You've got to be joking...' started Azra. 'You mean...?'

'Skala,' Sekobi nodded. 'Think about it, Azra. It's the one place the Baron can't touch us. The one place – right under his nose. There, we have wealth, we have our legacies.'

'*You* have wealth and legacies…' Azra said.

'I've spent years trying to run from it,' Quil said, sitting down at the table. 'But he's right. There are no other places to hide.'

And she looked at Azra. 'For you, perhaps, young thief, things are different … you have your skills, after all…'

'No! We stay together,' said Sylvindor, with surprising firmness. 'I'm not losing any more friends.'

Azra leaned back against the wall and rubbed her head. 'I don't get it. This is crazy. After all this, you just want to go back?!'

'*What other choice do we have?*' shouted Sekobi, slamming his hand on the table.

'And what do we do when we get to Skala?' Azra found herself shouting back. 'Just apologise to the Baron? Sorry we broke your Warren?'

Sekobi went to respond, then caught hold of himself, and exhaled a long breath.

'Whatever happens there,' Sekobi replied, in a quieter voice, 'at least it will be happening on our territory. The Warren is ours. Not just me and Quil. You too, Sylvindor, and you, Azra. Didn't you feel that much yourself?'

Azra reflected. 'But Syl – you can survive in the trees, surely? The Baron won't come for you there.'

Sylvindor clenched his teeth, then said: 'I need to see this through, Azra. I need to see the adventure through.'

Behind him, Azra could see Quil place her head in her hands.

'This is a ridiculous idea,' said Azra. 'How would you even get past the gates?'

There was a long silence. In the corner, Hathred lowered her head. Quil was closing and opening her fist, and Sekobi flicked small sparks from his fingers.

Like a weight sinking on her chest, it dawned on Azra.

'You want me to carry you in,' she said. 'Just like I took you out.'

'There'll be less goblins this time,' pointed out Sekobi, with the twisted smile he gave.

'It's a choice,' said Quil, finally. 'A decision for us all to make. And that decision remains open until the very gates themselves. But let's not fool ourselves. The decision is how to survive.' And then, resignedly, she pushed a sheet of parchment towards Azra. Azra could see that it was the same design the elf had shown her in Haemir. 'These are all over the place, you should know.'

Sylvindor swept the paper away.

'We beat the Baron's Rule of One by working together,' he declared. 'I say we do it again.'

Azra closed her eyes. 'It's a choice,' she said. 'I'll come with you.'

'Then we need to go now,' Sekobi said, and Azra heard the noise of the others getting up.

When she opened her eyes, only Hathred remained. And she looked at Azra sadly, and shook her head.

18

Return to Skala

They travelled by night, and all the time they had spent in the Warren together helped them cross the land under cover, avoiding patrols and the wandering eyes of other travellers, until once again the Screaming Mountains came into sight.

'They say the name comes from the wind, as it howls through the peaks and makes the noise of a scream,' said Quil. 'Although, I don't believe the noise was heard before the Baron opened the Warren.'

Sekobi was watching the gates of the citadel keenly. 'How close do we need to be?' he asked Azra.

She thought. *Closer than this.*

'We'll be seen by the guards if we get closer,' Quil said.

'Or by the queue,' said Sylvindor. 'They'll recognise Marsali Quil and Sekobi the Trickster straightaway.'

Azra scanned the ground before them, from their hiding place in a small thicket. 'There are some large rocks near the curtain wall,' she said. 'We could try two jumps. One to the rocks, then one into the citadel.'

'You don't sound convinced,' said Quil.

'Carrying all of us was ... exhausting, last time,' Azra admitted. 'I can take you one by one, perhaps.'

They all viewed the route being proposed. Quil turned around to the group.

'This is still a choice,' she said. 'We have no idea what will happen inside. And my guess is that it will not be pleasant.'

'We know what will happen *outside*,' said Sekobi, grittily.

'I'm just saying,' Quil said. 'I'm just ... it's a choice.' And she looked at Azra, in particular.

Azra did not return the look. Indeed, she was putting most thoughts out of her head.

'Are we ready?' she asked.

With that, she took hold of Sekobi's arm, and almost immediately they found themselves behind the smooth stone of the rocks, set in the ground just in front of the towering walls above them.

Sekobi peered around the side of the boulder, and then indicated to Azra to go back for the others. She vanished back into the thicket, where Quil was re-checking her sword.

'It all comes back to this,' she said, jadedly. 'Let's go.'

Azra and Quil arrived next to Sekobi, who was keeping a watch on the main gate.

'Just one more,' Azra whispered.

'Don't drop him,' Sekobi winked.

And then she was back at the hiding place. Sylvindor was clearly thinking of doing some of his exercises, but was also trying to stay low.

'Ready?' she asked.

'I think so,' he said. 'Do you know, I don't like how it feels when you do that vanishing thing. Turns the world all strange to me. But if this is the way in, it's the way in.'

And he breathed in a few times, preparing himself. Azra had been weighing things up in her mind, and realised that this was probably the last time she would get to say what she felt she needed to.

'Syl...' Azra said.

'Yes?'

'I—I just wanted to let you know. I've never had anyone look out for me before. You may be the first person I'd call a friend.'

Sylvindor's face lit up, but only for a moment. Then he looked strangely sad, as if remembering something. He struggled to find the words he was looking for.

'I know you don't trust people,' he said, eventually. 'But you know, not all people are bad. I know it seems that way sometimes, but not everyone is bad. Some people are afraid. Some people are hurt. But they aren't bad, Azra.'

Azra stood close to him. 'I admire that in you more than anything, Syl. More than your skills with a sword. You see the best in people. Even when there's not much to see.'

Sylvindor laughed a little. 'Oh, Azra. *You're* a good person! I know that much.'

Azra looked at the floor, then gently rested her hand on his shoulder.

'I think ... I think looking for the best in people will see you right. In the end.'

'What do you mean?'

Azra lifted her eyes to meet his. 'I have only done one good thing in my life, Sylvindor. And I've done it because you'll survive. Do you understand?'

Sylvindor shook his head. Azra's hand tightened into a grip.

'But you can't follow this madness. And that's why this is the one good thing I can do. Because I know you'll survive.'

As Sylvindor remained confused, Azra plunged her sword into his stomach. She held on as the air passed out of his body, then let the young elf's body slump to the floor.

She stood for a moment, harsh questions bombarding her brain, her hands itching, her sword suddenly heavy. Then, she vanished, back to the rocks.

'Where's the elf?' hissed Quil.

'He's not coming,' Azra replied. 'His choice was made.'

Sekobi went to say something, but Azra had regained focus, and without warning she clasped hold of both their arms, and the next moment they found themselves on a cobbled street of the citadel, the other side of the thick stone wall. Before they could get to their feet, or even get their bearings, they were met with a row of sharp spear points surrounding them.

'Welcome back to Skala,' said a guard. 'The Baron has been expecting you.'

19

The final confrontation

Azra, Quil and Sekobi found themselves standing in a large hall, with pillars on either side rising up to the exquisitely decorated ceiling high above. In between each pillar were several heavily armed guards, the Baron's finest warriors, surrounding the three adventurers. In front of them was a huge round table, covered in a cloth, and behind this a raised platform. On the platform, a man sat on a throne. He was powerful, dressed in a fine purple cloak, and adorned with gleaming golden chains and flashing diamond rings. Around him stood an array of servants and other members of his household behind him.

'I am so pleased you made it,' he said, in a large, booming voice. 'And I am delighted to finally make your acquaintance face to face. You will know me as the Baron Kaveshvill, and this is my palace.'

Azra stiffened, her eyes darting around the hall for any possible escape routes. There seemed to be very few. The pillars were smooth, the walls were manned by guards, and there seemed nowhere to vanish to at a short distance. There were not even light fittings for torches – indeed, it was not clear how the windowless hall was being lit at all.

'Let me bring in our final guest,' the Baron said, and clapped his hands together. Behind them, from the gate they had been brought through, there was a creaking sound, then the portcullis was raised, and three figures entered. Two were guards. The other, in between them, they recognised as the woman, Vane.

As she was marched past them, she whispered: 'Sorry.'

Vane was taken up to the platform, and the Baron invited her to take a smaller seat next to his throne.

'A pleasure to have you with us, my dear, for the end of this little adventure,' the Baron said. Then he turned back to the adventurers before him. 'You will, of course, have already met my daughter, Lagracia. Or whatever she calls herself these days.'

'Vane...' muttered Quil.

'Vane?' the Baron laughed, in an unkind way. 'After your mother, of course! I suspect you did not tell your new friends about our relationship when you sent them on this foolish errand. And I suspect that you, brave Marsali Quil, wily Sekobi the Trickster, and the vanishing girl, I suspect that you do not know that my daughter is quite unwell.'

'There is nothing wrong with me,' Vane said, quietly, keeping her poise on her seat, but with clear signs that she had suffered.

'Nonsense,' said the Baron. 'My daughter is afflicted by certain turns. You see, she blames me for the death of her mother, and she wishes some kind of revenge on me. Can you imagine! Her own father, who gave her so much.'

'You locked me in a tower, father,' replied Vane, coldly. 'You gave me only reasons to destroy you.'

The Baron ignored her. 'But only while you were ill, my dear. And when we graciously received you back here in Skala, I gave you money, power ... and even access to my library. Foolishly, she took it upon herself to remove several maps recently – thinking I would not notice!'

So that's where she got the maps from, Azra thought.

'So you see, it was not long before I understood her plans to breach the Warren,' the Baron continued. 'And with a little persuasion...' – at this, Vane winced – 'I soon gathered the full extent of her ambition. I must say, bringing back two of the greatest warriors the Warren has ever known was a touch of genius, dear. I see you have inherited at least something from me.'

The Baron stood up. 'I hope my Warren provided the challenge you all expected,' he said, curling his lip. 'I did try to make you feel so very ... welcome.'

'What do you mean?' asked Quil, determinedly.

'Such an honour to have the two legends back here in Skala! Especially when we all thought at least one of you was no more. I wouldn't have wanted you to move too far off the beaten track, as it were. It would have made you less easy to see.'

He clapped his hands again, and four servants ran forward and removed the cloth from the top of the table. To Azra's surprise, she saw it was a mirror – a huge mirror, reflecting off another above it. The Baron coughed, then moved a lever with his hand, adjusting the angle. The image on the mirror moved, blurring slightly over lines and circles, until it was brought to focus on what must have been a top-down view of what seemed like an empty plaza. There were things strewn all around it, and in the middle was a skeleton, with bright, green boots...

'You were ... watching? All the time?' Quil couldn't believe it. Her exclamation made the Baron laugh, cruelly.

'Of course. How else would I and my household enjoy the Warren? I'm not going to go down there, am I? And once there was the prospect of the great Marsali Quil and Sekobi the Trickster coming back – one last time, so they said – well, I wanted to ensure there was a spectacle!'

'The lower levels,' Sekobi said, grinding his jaw. 'They were empty because you cleared them.'

'Not something I would normally do, I must admit. But I did find the performance enjoyable. You know, goblins aren't the best fighters, but they are the most pliable. Poor Moshab realised that, of course, but what he didn't realise was pliable works both ways. I made sure he failed...'

'But *we* didn't fail,' said Quil. 'We beat your goblins.'

'Indeed, and it was *exciting!*' cried the Baron, looking to his assembled household and guards for agreement. 'And a crying shame that you used some kind of fog trick, Sekobi. After all, we were all so sad when the elf died. Were we not?'

Around him, the Baron's household staff made appropriately emotional noises.

'But it added to the drama so much!' The Baron threw his hands up triumphantly.

Sekobi looked puzzled. 'There was no trick...' he began. Then he looked at Azra, and she back at him, and they all realised that somehow the mirror's view had been blocked before Sylvindor had recovered. The Baron thought him dead.

Could it be, Azra thought, could it be when she vanished to start the fire...? Just as Hathred had described, bending reality?

'Of course, we all wanted to see you take on the dragon,' the Baron continued. 'But mirrors can only reach so far down. The goblins were meant to bring you back to the plaza here, but it seems they weren't up to the job. Nevertheless! I am pleased that you have all returned to give the crowd one final performance!'

Quil stepped forward. 'Performance? No. We're through with your games.'

The Baron laughed.

'Are you? Yet here you are. Back in Skala, back with your swords and magic. Such a coincidence that you all had the idea to come back to my domain, though,' he said, stroking his chin. 'Tell me, who first suggested it?'

Azra looked up at Quil. She had her eyes fixed on the Baron, a stare with such hatred and loathing. She looked at Sekobi, who's dark eyes were burning like flames.

'Or ... perhaps you all did?' he laughed again. 'So amusing to me how heroic adventurers' wills can be bent on the promise of gold, the promise of freedom – or even the promise of the same Warren they wanted to steal from.'

And Azra looked again at her fellow adventurers, and saw their faces, and realised that they had all suggested they come back. All of them except her. And she had not opened the second letter...

The Baron sat back down in his chair.

'The game is not over, Marsali Quil,' he said, in an icy voice. 'Because the Rule of One is not satisfied. To finish the game, there can only be one. As my letters made clear. You see, once I became aware of my daughter's little ... game, I had to put certain fail-safes in place. The first was, of course, the goblin ambush. So I could draw you out, see the full extent of your group. The second was the dragon – I did suspect this would be the end of you, I must admit. I then had my men posted on the cave entrance to ensure the gold ended up back where it belonged, and all of you too. But knowing of your legendary ways, I also had one last fail-safe. A letter sent to our adventurers, such that they might find them on their return should they escape my guards. And each letter promised them their heart's desires, on one condition. That they bring the others back here, to Skala. Back here, to me. Of course, I sent the letters before the young elf passed away. Such a shame! Because if that was not the case, we could have a proper melee!'

The Baron watched the adventurers look at each other, realising what he was ordering.

'You want us to fight – *each other*?' Azra asked.

The Baron was amused. 'That is the Rule of One, my dear. Is it not? You will fight to the death, and the winner will take all. But here, I am a charitable sort. And I recognise that these others are far superior to you, little vanisher, in experience and abilities. No doubt, given the chance, they would both round on you first. Get you out of the way, if you follow me.'

'That's not true!' said Quil, furiously.

'Ah, but Marsali Quil, would I be so cruel? Where would the entertainment be? And I am so fascinated by this girl's ... special tricks.'

The Baron spoke to his household, and to the guards all around. 'So you see, here is the final confrontation. Quil against Sekobi. I will spare the vanisher's life. Oh, the vanisher will have to fight ... this is the brilliance of it all. It all comes down to this little thief deciding on who to side with first. You see, my girl, you must decide which one you will fight with. And which one you will ... try ... to kill. Perhaps we will see the greatness of Marsali Quil's sword in defeating two arch-rivals! Perhaps Sekobi will outwit them both! Only one thing is for certain: there can only be one of them left standing. Their prize will be what was promised to them in their letters. Except the vanisher, who will remain here – as my guest. And in this way, your attempt to 'beat' my Warren will fail on its very premise. The Rule of One cannot be defeated.'

Then the Baron sat down. 'So much more of a game, this way. Who will she choose?'

'Why should I do this?' asked Azra.

The Baron reclined. 'Because all you have is your life, and your life is only worth something while *I* find it valuable. You have nothing else, girl. No other choices. Nothing at all. You have no gold. You have no glory. Your friends all betrayed you. Your only option now is to fight.'

But quite unexpectedly, Azra smiled. And she looked at Quil, and she looked at Sekobi, and then back to the Baron, and she smiled again, a kind of twisted half-smile that Sekobi so often used.

'You're wrong,' she said. 'I do have gold. Gold taken from your Warren. More gold than anyone might ever need out there, out in the world.'

'That's not possible,' replied the Baron. 'I know exactly how things played out when you attempted to leave the Warren. You found the so-called magic door too ancient to open. So you, young vanisher, transported the treasure, along with your companions. A very impressive feat, may I say. But once you had broken your way through the bricked-up cave wall, you were attacked before you could move any from out of the cave. You ran, all of you, leaving all your reward behind for my men to seize. And, may I say, a very fine addition to my treasury that gold is.'

Sekobi was staring at her.

'No,' he said, as if an image were forming in his head, a reconfiguring of memories that he had previously accepted but now challenged. 'No, it didn't happen like that.'

'What? Then do pray tell how it did, Master Sekobi.'

'She took the first two chests. But she was gone for a long time. I thought she may have even run off with them. But, of course, two would have been too much to carry for one girl.'

Quil closed her eyes. 'And she came back for the other two ... but when we got to the cave...'

'What do you mean, four chests?' demanded the Baron, bringing his fist down on his chair arm. 'There were only *three* chests of treasure!'

Sekobi put his head back. 'There were three chests in the cave. The fourth, the vanisher took. Having blindly vanished once, she perhaps took one more risk and aimed for the outside. Your guards wouldn't have seen her, it would have been too quick, Baron. But she would have seen they were there.'

Azra did not go against anything Sekobi said. In fact, she nodded her head. 'Yes. I hid the first chest where nobody would see it, just outside of the cave's entrance. Where I saw the Baron's guards in disguise, though I wasn't sure for certain if they were simply Vane's men.'

'Then you came back into the cave – but perhaps seeing the guards you were unsettled, and you vanished too short a distance.'

'Yes, I appeared outside of the bricked-up wall. I'd gone straight past it the first time. Now I was on the wrong side.'

'So you knocked the bricks out. Just enough for you to crawl back through.'

Azra folded her arms. 'You would have done the same. Both of you.'

Quil stepped forward. 'You can't say that. You can't know that.'

'I can, because we're all here,' Azra replied. 'You both read the letters and you both acted. So I do know it.'

And she turned away from Quil, with an emotion she had never felt before surging into her chest. It was one of sadness, because she did not want to leave Quil or Sekobi, but it was also determination, because of what they had taught her, and what it turned out they had done to her. She focused straight at the Baron.

'I don't think I will be playing this game, Baron. Before going back to Blackwater I got the chest and moved it to somewhere far more secure, where I will be able to live off it for the rest of my life.' Then she shot a look at both of her former companions and added: 'The way *I* decide to.'

The Baron was livid. He called for his guards, who encircled the adventurers.

'Kill them! Kill them all!'

But Azra kept focused on the Baron. And as she did, the audience began to feel the chamber tremble, then shake, then rock. And as the energy swarmed into Azra's body, she projected a leap straight into the Baron's mirror, which shattered into a thousand pieces, sending shards of glass hurtling in every direction.

The crowd shrieked and gasped, and many took cover, while others fled. The guards backed away, exchanging uncertain glances and clearly not wanting to approach this powerful new magic.

The shaking subsided. Azra straightened herself up. Then she turned to the gate they had entered through, and calmly walked up to it. She looked at the guards, pointing their spears at her, and waited for them to slowly lower their weapons. The gate opened, and Azra walked out – leaving Skala and the Warren once and for all.

Or so she thought.

JUVENILE FICTION, NON-FICTION, PARENTING

Our Street Books are for children of all ages, delivering a potent
mix of fantastic, rip-roaring adventure and fantasy stories to
excite the imagination; spiritual fiction to help the mind and the
heart; humorous stories to make the funny bone grow;
historical tales to evolve interest; and all manner of subjects that
stretch imagination, grab attention, inform, inspire and keep
the pages turning. Our subjects include Non-fiction and Fiction,
Fantasy and Science Fiction, Religious, Spiritual, Historical,
Adventure, Social Issues, Humour, Folk Tales and more.
If you have enjoyed this book, why not tell other readers by
posting a review on your preferred book site.

Recent bestsellers from Our Street Books are:

Relax Kids: Aladdin's Magic Carpet
Marneta Viegas
Let Snow White, the Wizard of Oz and other fairytale
characters show you and your child how to meditate and relax.
Meditations for young children aged 5 and up.
Paperback: 978-1-78279-869-9 Hardcover: 978-1-90381-666-0

Wonderful Earth
An interactive book for hours of fun learning
Mick Inkpen, Nick Butterworth
An interactive Creation story: Lift the flap,
turn the wheel, look in the mirror, and more.
Hardcover: 978-1-84694-314-0

Boring Bible: Super Son Series 1
Andy Robb
Find out about angels, sin and the Super Son of God.
Paperback: 978-1-84694-386-7

Jonah and the Last Great Dragon
Legend of the Heart Eaters
M.E. Holley
When legendary creatures invade our world,
only dragon-fire can destroy them; and
Jonah alone can control the Great Dragon.
Paperback: 978-1-78099-541-0 ebook: 978-1-78099-542-7

Little Prayers Series: Classic Children's Prayers
Alan and Linda Parry
Traditional prayers told by your child's favourite creatures.
Hardcover: 978-1-84694-449-9

Magnificent Me, Magnificent You – The Grand Canyon
Dawattie Basdeo, Angela Cutler
A treasure-filled story of discovery with a range of
inspiring fun exercises, activities, songs and games
for children aged 6 to 11.
Paperback: 978-1-78279-819-4

Q is for Question
An ABC of Philosophy
Tiffany Poirier
An illustrated non-fiction philosophy book to help
children aged 8 to 11 discover, debate and articulate
thought-provoking, open-ended questions about
existence, free will and happiness.
Hardcover: 978-1-84694-183-2

Relax Kids: How to be Happy
52 positive activities for children
Marneta Viegas
Fun activities to bring the family together.
Paperback: 978-1-78279-162-1

Rise of the Shadow Stealers
The Firebird Chronicles
Daniel Ingram-Brown
Memories are going missing. Can Fletcher and
Scoop unearth their own lost history and save the
Storyteller's treasure from the shadows?
Paperback: 978-1-78099-694-3 ebook: 978-1-78099-693-6

Readers of ebooks can buy or view any of these bestsellers by clicking on the live link in the title. Most titles are published in paperback and as an ebook. Paperbacks are available in traditional bookshops. Both print and ebook formats are available online.

Find more titles and sign up to our readers' newsletter at www.collectiveinkbooks.com/children-and-young-adult